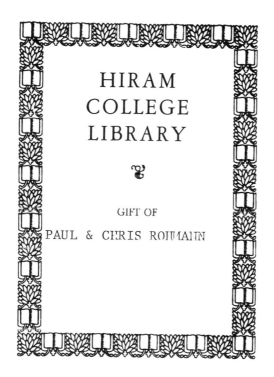

QUETZALCOATL

QUETZALCOATL

A NOVEL BY

José Lopez Portillo

TRANSLATED FROM THE SPANISH BY

Eliot Weinberger & Diana S. Goodrich

A CONTINUUM BOOK

THE SEABURY PRESS ● NEW YORK

1976
The Seabury Press
815 Second Avenue
New York, New York 10017

Printed in the United States of America

Library of Congress Cataloging in Publication Data

Lopez-Portillo y Pacheco, José.
Quetzalcoatl.
(A Continuum book)
1. Quetzalcoatl—Fiction. I. Title.
PZ4.L864Qe3   [PQ7298.22.06]   863   76-25163
ISBN 0-8164-9303-0

CONTENTS

QUETZALCOATL

In the Beginning

O MEYOCAN! I will go back to the second place, the place of Wind and Darkness, the *Yoalli Ehecatl,* where the infinite stillness swirls around before the unifying will of the Word.

"I am there. Am I someone?" My spirit speaks.

"I am there. Am I the one I am?"

Before time, in a point without space, in the dark whirl-pool, in the navel where the infinitely great becomes the infinitely small, in the navel where the Diverse becomes the Universe, where the *Tloque Nahuaque* is the night storm of the potential, where the Lord of Night, black Tezcatlipoca, negates himself, the universe that Quetzalcoatl (the precious twin, the feather on the scale) wants to create is born, bursting into light. I crawl and I fly. Eagle and serpent.

Suns were created.

Feathers were created.

Tigers were created.

Songs were created.

Grief began and blood was throbbing.

"I am the one who is," said the Word.
"I know what I am," said man.

And he left the hands of his Creator and remained in his own care.
Yoalli Ehecatl.
Wind and Darkness!

CHAPTER I

❧

The Way

THE DARK NIGHT, the wind and the sea cast him on the beach. He remained enchained, tied to his cross, covered with foam, stuck to the earth, clinging to its loving shape like a child to its mother.

Naked and without memory. His endurance shone from within him like a star in the wind and darkness. Light within. And outside, the storm and the whirlpool roared.

The calm and the first light of a new day found him lying on the beach. He could only remember the course of his origin, the sun coming out, and the cross of the four winds to which he was tied, the cross which carried him, afloat on the sea, through howling storms and up on to this earth, separated from the water, surrounded by wind and night.

He was naked, without memory, with only the will to survive. He was crazed with need. His heart was full of anguish and solitude.

"Am I still someone?" he was scarcely able to ask himself as pain hurled him against the rocks, and his strength and consciousness left him, the sparkle of his endurance died, and the only thing left was a grey humming, like death, which tasted in his swollen mouth like blood and salt.

He remained on the ground, stuck like a flint, covered with white and scaly foam, his stomach pressed to the earth.

The new day came from the sea. The new day full of light.

The light woke birds and song. The new day had songs and shining feathers. Birds came and perched on his tangled and matted beard, on his arms, his back, and on his cross, and yet he did not awaken.

From a distance, in that morning light, he looked like a plumed serpent come from the sea, from where the sun rises. And the children shouted to their elders:

"The sun brought a plumed serpent!"

"It's lying on the beach and only its feathers are moving!"

But the men paid no attention. They were too busy hunting food for their children.

Only children have the curiosity and the time to examine plumed serpents on a beach. And they went to see it more closely. They approached little by little, cautious and with fear. They looked at one another. Then the most daring of them ran toward it, stumbled, and startled the birds, their flight reawakening the fear of birds in the children's hearts.

"He has become a man! A white man! He has a hairy face and body!"

They ran to hide in the humid, foetid mass of the jungle.

"The plumed serpent has become a man! A white and hairy man!" They shouted to the men again, and again they were ignored. The men were busy and not curious. They caught lizards, small animals, and birds with their stones and sticks.

The children went back to the beach. Now they too took sticks and stones.

Now he was only a naked and strange man lying on the beach and tied to a piece of wood. He was motionless. They threw stones at him from afar. Moving closer, they hit him, and the most daring poked him until he bled.

The brilliant red blood trickled to the ground, and the ground drank it for the first time.

He raised his head and opened his large round eyes.

"God! God!" he shouted hoarsely through his tangled beard. He had a vague, burning, dazzled vision of the little dark brown figures that, frightened, ran to their elders to tell them of their feat.

"He has the round eyes of a serpent and a lot of hair on his face!"

Only Acatl was interested. He knew that the sea was generous and that sometimes it threw good things on the beach.

He scared the children away so that they would not come back, and at sunset he went to look for the plumed serpent. Perhaps he would be able to eat it. Perhaps he would adorn himself with its feathers.

When he arrived at the place, he too startled the birds and discovered the bearded, naked, white body of a man who was nearly dead, who had a trace of dry blood on his side.

"Hey! Hey! Who are you? Why are you white and bearded? Where do you come from? Are you a god? Are you dead?" He poked him with his spear, and the man moved.

"You were brought by the sea, the sun, and the wind.

"You must be a seed that has come from far away.

"You must be a spore from other lands.

"You must be the beginning of another race."

He untied him from the wood and, grabbing him by his hair and beard, dragged him with great difficulty toward the thicket. His feet made twin lines that began at the abandoned cross.

A new pain wrenched him from unconsciousness. He lacked the strength to complain. He couldn't even bite the dark and sweaty arm that clasped his head and pressed his dry mouth against his teeth. He let himself be dragged.

Through his swollen eyes, his need and his pain, he could see the evening star shining as his endurance had shone through the stormy nights. He was unaware that the evening star was beautiful. He only knew that it was still shining, as his own existence still shone.

"God! I am still me!" he managed to say. "I am still suffering! I can still see the evening star! You have not abandoned me! I am still pain and light!"

The dark man released him, panting, by the fresh water. As the fallen man drank water from his hand, Acatl had the unforgettable sensation of thick and sticky hair, and the brilliance of an eye where twilight and the evening star were reflected.

"He is thirsty. He is big and heavy. Perhaps he is a defeated god. Perhaps he is the seed of a god who is going to be born. Perhaps he is merely a suffering man."

For seven days he brought him food and drink and kept him hidden in a cave.

On the eighth day he did not find him, and he became sad. He was humiliated. He went back to his village.

"What have you done with the plumed serpent?" they asked him. "You were lost for seven days! The children saw you going for the serpent. You frightened them. You wanted it for yourself! Did you eat it all by yourself? Do you not have a people with whom to eat? The wise men beyond the hill say that wonders have been seen on the sea.

We have seen a serpent of light in the heavens. We think it is its mother in search of her child.

"What have you done with the serpent? Do you worship it by yourself? Do you not have a people with whom to worship? Do you think of yourself as a new man? Do you think gods are worshipped alone, without people and without sacrifices?

"Look here! Do not anger us any more! Bring the plumed serpent! It belongs to this land and to this air!"

Then Acatl said, "He has gone. He has vanished. For seven days I gave him water, honey, and fruit. Now he has gone. Now I am alone in front of you. I myself dragged the serpent. I grabbed it by its hair and it became a white and bearded man. I think it was only a man."

"Don't lie to us! Go and bring it or we'll beat you to death!"

Acatl went with pain in his heart. He ran to the sea and ran along the shore until he was exhausted. Squatting, facing the east, he ate nothing for two days. Devotion was being born in his heart.

Every night he saw the serpent of light in the sky. During the day he looked for the serpent on the land and could not find it. He could see the sun rise from its bloody struggle against the dead of Mictlan, and the crimson victory in its single eye which soon became dazzling.

For two days he did not eat. At the first light of the third day he saw him shining in the distance among the waves. He was tossing a sort of cobweb into the sea, and in it fish were caught. Part of his body was covered, and once again his beard was full of foam.

Acatl waited for the sun to come out and then appeared

7

before him. Suddenly he found himself wrapped in the web and in laughter, and he was knocked down.

"You are a man who knows how to laugh.

"You are a man who knows how to fish with cobwebs.

"You could not be a god.

"I have come for you. My people claim you are a plumed serpent.

"They say that the earth and skies want you."

The fisherman said nothing. He only laughed harder. He took Acatl, entangled, far away to a shady grove. He lit a fire and shared the fish with him.

They were together for a year.

Acatl learned new and surprising things. The other man learned how to speak and he found out about the things of the earth.

"I have a great deal to do.

"I have a great deal to give.

"I feel strong.

"I feel like a river.

"I feel like a road. I know, and do not remember.

"In some place there is a lord from whom I am sent. I am to give. I am to flow. I am to lead. I am to save myself."

At the year's end, he buried his cross and prepared to set out. Acatl was to announce his arrival at the first village, which was his own.

They came out of their huts to look at his robes, his nets, and the banner he was waving.

"Acatl is back, but without the serpent," the women shrieked.

"Acatl is back as if he were a lord," shouted the young men.

"You come as if you knew, you come as if you were announcing something," the old men observed.

"I am announcing the serpent. The time has come for him to teach. Get ready to receive him. Let there be a feast. He is a man who knows. He is good. He teaches new things. He does good things. Let there be a feast. He does not come as a serpent, he comes as a man."

"You are lying. Your soul is full of malice and your body full of pride. You think you are different. You think of yourself as an eagle. You announce this coming and yet you do not bring a token. You have not heeded our warnings. You have hidden for a year."

The old women stripped him of his ornaments. The young men took his banner. The old men cried, "Imprison him! Let him die tomorrow before the sun comes up. Let his blood be his last nourishment. Let him remain naked and bare. Strip the pride from his body."

"I must not die," Acatl said. "I already know things. I want to announce the good things that my lord will give. I do not want to die. I want to be a witness to the new age."

"You will die," said the old men. "That way you will be useful. Your death is good. It maintains the juice of the world. You will sustain the course of the evening stars and will make the sun firmly rooted in the sky."

"My blood will be useless if you take it from me. The white man knows that only blood that is given willingly pleases the gods. He told me this and I believe him. I shall not give my blood. The time has not yet come. I do not accept my death. I do not want it."

"Blood is blood," the old men replied. "Your will is yours, keep it. When you die, you will be the shadow of your shadow. You will want nothing then because you will no longer have blood. We want your death, we give your blood, that is the will of the people, that is the will that counts."

"It will be as it must," said Acatl, and he was locked up.

"Now I fear death. Before I only feared pain. He taught me to fear death if it is not accepted. 'You are free and you can be immortal,' he said to me. 'You have the will to accept. You can choose between resignation and fear. I did not want to die, and many nights the storm roared until it drove me mad. It deprived me of my reason, but not of my will, and I did not want to die. I want to be the way. And I shall die when I want to.'

"I am free and yet I am imprisoned," Acatl thought.

"I want to live and they are going to kill me.

"I do not understand. A short time ago my world was simple. Now I know, and I have doubts. I believe, and I falter. Now I know that my will sins and my innocence is not happy. My body is anguished with pain and my soul with death. Sometimes I think I should not have fed him, and yet I believe I only want to live to announce his coming. I do not understand. It will be as it will. I shall know tomorrow."

Today became tomorrow, and Acatl did not die.

What happened was that he arrived and destroyed the god who would have tasted Acatl's blood.

And the heavens did not fall, and it only rained, and the sun shone in spite of everything. They allowed him to speak.

It happened like this.

He came with his feathered cloak, adorned with crosses. Tall, bearded, strong, alone.

He came slowly and with open arms.

10

He came with his round eyes.

He came with a strong wind at his back which stirred his cloak as if it were burning, as if it were in flames. And he shouted with his great voice:

"Where is my herald?

"Where is the one who announces me?

"I want to see him! Bring him to me at once!"

"Today they will sacrifice him to the gods!" the boy who had made him bleed cried joyfully.

"He shall not die!" shouted the man.

"I do not want him to die. His time will come. Give him to me."

The oldest man among them emerged from the silence and the fear and, with a firm voice that filled his sons and grandsons with pride, said:

"You have just arrived and already you are shouting.

"You have just arrived and already you are giving orders.

"Who are you? Who do you think you are?"

"I do not know who I am, but I have come to give."

"And who asks you to? Who knows you?

"We have awaited a plumed serpent for a year, from the time when its mother was in the sky, and you did not come then. You hid in the jungle, like a fugitive. You stole a man away from us. You deprived him of his reason, reason given to him by this people, and now he says he does not want to die. He says he is free. We wanted a plumed serpent and you come as a bearded man, shouting. Your round eyes give out flames of madness and you frighten the children. I myself am frightened because we have never seen one like you before. We do not know where you come from or where you are to go. We do not know if you are someone. We do not know if you are fruit or seed. We do not know if you belong to the earth or to the sky."

11

"I am made of earth and I wish to reach the heavens. I am scales and wish to be wings. I need to flow, I must give. Help me give and I will go to the sky."

"You say strange things," said the elder. "What will you give us?"

"I will give your souls the science of sin and of redemption, and I will teach you the science of the earth to improve your lives."

"What you say is truly strange. I want nothing of what you promise. There are gods on our altars already, and a sun in our world. They provide our nourishment and we provide theirs. We already have those who give to us and to whom we give. Our lives already flow. My own will soon arrive at its shadow. We ask nothing of you. And what do you ask for in exchange?"

"Give Acatl to me. The hour of his death has not come. He has already learned, he is already free."

"There are orders for his death. The god awaits it."

"And where is he who awaits the death of a free man?"

"Up there. Acatl will die at his feet, as do the chosen ones on this earth, so that the sun will continue to rise. Everything has been prepared. It will be so."

"The sun will rise and Acatl will not die!" shouted the man.

Then a great wind blew from the sea and the heavens rumbled with thunder.

He strode up the steps, his cloak flapping like an eagle's wing. Some thought he was flying, and were frightened even more. He enveloped the god in his net and pulled until it was demolished. It was broken into five pieces. Each piece struck each of the five priests, knocked them down the steps and killed them.

"The sun will rise from the east!"

And the sun rose from the east while a strong rain fell.

"You are powerful!" the old men cried.

"You destroyed our god! You brought wind and then water! The god fell and the sun rose from the east!

"We no longer have a god.

"Stay with us. You will be the new god. We will feed you blood so that you may maintain your great strength and increase your great power. You will be Quetzalcoatl!"

"I cannot be a god. I am barely a man and I have already sinned. I do not want blood. I have come to give my own. I am a man who wants to save and to save himself. I want to give and I have already killed."

And he walked away and made himself bleed and slowly went down the steps.

"Here is my blood! Here is my blood!" he shouted feverishly, splattering the stunned people while the women screamed.

"I shall pay for my guilt! I killed five to save one! I will shed my blood! I fell to the temptation of violence! I killed! I killed!" And he implored the people:

"Forgive me! Forgive me!"

"What are we to forgive you for?" the old men asked.

"My sin. I have killed five men."

"And what is sin?" they asked.

"To sin is to disobey the command of God in heart and in deed."

"We do not understand. The commands of gods are always fulfilled. They want death. They are gods of death who must be served. We do not know what it is to sin. To kill is to comply with death. They created it. They cultivated it. What can we do against the gods? Nothing is done unless they will it. We are here under the law of life created by the gods."

13

Acatl had risen from the sacrificial stone to which he had been tied by the priests. He cried:

"My lord has sinned to save me. He must love me a great deal to sin for me. I will follow him. I will serve him. My lord has sinned."

"Stay and perhaps we shall learn how to sin," the old men said to him. "And then perhaps we shall know how to pardon you."

"No," he said, "I could not live here where I have killed. I could have no tranquillity where there is no pardon. I shall go on my way. I shall go to the mountains. I shall do penance there. And then I shall resolve what to do with my life."

"If you must," the old men said, resigning themselves. "But do not go alone. Let someone go to serve you. Let him be your witness. Take Acatl with you."

"I want to go with the serpent too," begged the boy who had made him bleed.

"You may go in peace, Tatle, if he wants you," the old men agreed.

"Let him come with me," he said. "He will help me do penance. He already knows the color of my blood."

And so began his journey to the plateau. To the high plateau of Anahuac.

In this way he began to build his retinue, men who would always accompany him and who would later be called "Cocomes." He was past the age of thirty then, and he had forgotten his name and his origins. He knew only his own condition.

"They call me Quetzalcoatl and from now on and forever, that will be my name.

"I am Quetzalcoatl.

14

"I am the plumed serpent. I crawl and I fly. Earth and air. Mud and sky. I have fallen and I will rise.

"Thus will they know me. Thus will they remember me. I am Quetzalcoatl."

The people begged him, "Leave us a sign."

And Quetzalcoatl planted a cross in the ground and said, "This is the true Tree of the Universe."

And he left without saying another word, followed by Acatl and Tatle, while the people stood watching him in silence, surprise, and reverence until he was out of sight.

"He is truly a strange being. He announces a new age. The people of Anahuac will weep greatly," the oldest one declared. "He will be yeast. He will be joy and bitterness for the people of the plateau. He has already passed through here and has taken a god from us. He has left us a tree, five dead, words we do not understand, and much confusion. Our people will no longer be as they have been."

For two days he walked barefoot, without food. He carried Tatle on his shoulders when he saw the boy was tired. For two days he did not speak a word. Only walking, walking, walking, until he attained the simple ecstasy of walking which comes prior to the ecstasy of dancing. The flight of elementary rhythm, one two, one two, repeated until the step takes over the body, fixes itself in the heart, empties the head, and lets everything be forgotten. One two, one two. Measuring the earth, caressing it, rejoicing in its gravity. Walking, walking, walking. At night, with the moon and the silence, in the fragrance, in the elementary ecstasy

15

of rhythm one two that fuses earth, man, and the infinite in a semispherical horizon, always in flight.

For two days they walked until they came to the mountains that shelter Citlaltepetl and its eternal snows, high and pure as a star.

"They will come for me in fifteen days. Go ahead and announce my coming. Talk, tell, explain. Prepare. Let there be feasting and no death."

And for fifteen days he fasted and did penance to redeem his guilt through his own pain.

CHAPTER II

❧

Anahuac

AFTER those fifteen days had passed, they came back
for him.

Many came. Important people and common people.

Acatl and Tatle stepped forward:

"Fifteen days have gone by. We are here as you ordered.
We have complied with your wishes. We have spoken to the
people, announcing your coming, carrying your sign, the
Tree of the Universe. Many want to know you and have
come for you. They want you to teach them. They know of
your great knowledge and of your power. Your fame precedes you because it is known that you destroy gods and that
you are even willing to kill because you do not want death.
It is known that you say you will make our lives better."

"Come here, for I can barely move after these days of fasting and penance. I have suffered and now I am pure. Now I
can face other men."

They all went to him and remained for a long while, until
he opened his eyes and stood up, helped by Acatl and Tatle.

"I an Quetzalcoatl," he said. "I do not know which is my
land. I only know that I come from where the sun rises. I

come to make this earth, and thus myself, better. I am between two spheres and I love earth and sky equally well. I want to plant the four boughs of the Tree of the Universe to strengthen the union between the earth and the sky. I want to make men better so that they may find the lord I serve, the lord whose name I cannot remember. I do not want to fall into temptation."

"Speak for us," the people told Topiltzin, "you, who always ask questions."

And Topiltzin said:

"We know what your name is but not who you are. It is not important where you came from. What matters is where you wish to go. They say that you fell like an arrow shot by the night storm, and that now you are among us. We understand little of what you say. We wish to hear your words and to know your deeds. So doing, you will give us something. Come with us. Build your house among us. We shall give you women and servants. You will give us your sons so that they may enrich the blood of our people."

"I shall go with you. I shall build a house among you, with many rooms. But I shall take no woman. I must not indulge in the flesh nor take pride in my lineage. You will all be my sons. I shall love you as such. So it must be."

"So will it be if you wish it," they replied. "You will explain your words so that we may understand."

And because he was weak and his feet were swollen, he was carried on the shoulders of four porters. So they began their journey to Anahuac. He announced his presence to the people, and they came to greet him with joy.

"Quetzalcoatl has come! He announces a new age for Anahuac! Let him be welcome. Let us make his time here pleasant."

And they took flowers and feathers to him.

18

And thus he arrived in Tula. Quetzalcoatl saw the vastness, the beauty, and the richness of the land.

"This is where I shall rule. This is where I shall build. This is where I shall create," he said to himself. And he thanked the one above. He saw the many people that lived in the land.

"They will all be my brothers. They will be my children. I will rule over them," he told himself. "I shall change their customs. I shall change their gods and their rites. I shall make them all equal. I shall make them rich, free, and gentle."

They gave him a hut to live in, for the men from Tula only knew how to build huts of sticks and straw. And as servants they gave him, along with Acatl and Tatle, the four porters that had carried him on the road, as he had requested.

He did not go out the first day. He was meditating. On the second day he went out with only Tatle, whom he held by the hand. He went around the city without speaking to anyone. He was draped in a great brilliant feathered cape which he had made along the way, and which hung from his shoulders and dragged on the ground. His walk was slow and dignified. He made a display of his great height, and indeed he looked like a god walking with a small dark naked man at his side.

They all watched and admired him.

"This Quetzalcoatl is big, strong, white, bearded," the people commented. "He will live among us."

And many people followed him silently until he returned to his hut.

🌷

On the third day there was a feast in the village. They were planning to sacrifice two prisoners, two savage Chichimecs who had been captured in the mountain wars and who could hardly speak. The morning came with a great beating of sticks against tree trunks as the people were called to witness this sacrifice to the gods according to the accepted rite. Four priests would hold them by their hands and feet. And then they would hurl them against a large stone, smashing their backs and chests until they were split apart. Then, using flint knives, a fifth priest would cut away the ribs and tear out their hearts. And while their hearts were still beating, he would present them to the god, who would consume this most exquisite food of the universe, the blood from the best of created beings, man, whom all others serve and provide with nourishment. The ceremony had been prepared and everything was ready. They only waited for the sunrise.

Screaming and sobbing, the victims attempted to defend themselves, and had to be dragged and beaten amidst the laughter of the people. In this manner they were taken to the temple.

Then Quetzalcoatl appeared, and once again extended his arms and slowly walked to where the sacrifice was about to take place.

"Brothers! Brothers!" he cried in his great thundering voice.

They all became quiet.

"I am Quetzalcoatl, and two things will I teach today:

"First, no one has the right to spill more than his own blood.

"Second, I shall make your sticks more sonorous so that they will sing."

The priests, who were struggling with the prisoners, expressed their displeasure.

"Do not let the ritual be interrupted! The wrath of the gods will come! Let the act be carried out as usual! As our forefathers taught us! Its order must be maintained! The world must be made firm!"

"That is not the order of the world!" said Quetzalcoatl. "I represent a different one. But this is not to be discussed now. I only ask that the sacrifice be postponed till midday while I make the wood sing."

"Let it be so," said the leaders.

"No!" the priests protested.

"Let it be so!" said the people, whose adoration was for Quetzalcoatl alone.

Quetzalcoatl took off his cloak and began to work in front of everyone. He used flint knives and a fire which he himself lit. He chose a beautiful tree trunk and, cutting here and burning there, hollowed it out and made, before midday, two vibrating tongues which he rhythmically began to play.

"In truth he has taught the wood to sing," the people said, hearing the rhythmical sound. "In truth he knows how to do beautiful things."

Quetzalcoatl went on playing the *teponaxtle*.

The sonorous rhythm soon turned into a dance beat, and the people began to dance without noticing the sun, which rose and set. The dance became a collective ecstasy. The people forgot death, and their hearts were filled with the song of the wood, which only stopped when night set in.

Then Quetzalcoatl said:

"Brothers, the dance of the people is more pleasing to the lord than the death of a miserable person. Music makes the spheres turn. The entire universe moves to a beat. Let us take the rhythm of the stars and learn the rotation of the sun. Out of each beat of the rhythm, let us make our own space. Let us dance as the constellations dance. Let us fuse ourselves with the total rhythm of the universe, and in this way we shall rise to the lord and our steps will be pleasing to him, for we shall be constructing fleeting universes of beauty."

And he played the *teponaxtle* again.

Then the priests cried:

"Be damned! Damnation for this dull people who abandon their gods! They have interrupted the sound, the tradition of blood, for too long. The sun is already in Mictlan and it needs the blood of man to shine with strength tomorrow. It is not music that stops the sun, it is blood that sustains it!"

Tired of dancing, the people hesitated. Then Quetzalcoatl cried:

"Here is my blood! I give it to you doubting people so that no more brothers will be sacrificed." And he opened his wounds and they began to flow until dark stains covered the ground.

"This is my blood. I shed it of my own will so that the blood of my fellow beings will not be spilled.

"And this is the other lesson that I wanted to give to you before the night ends: that no more pain be caused other than that which is accepted. Only one's own blood may be shed. I shall spill my blood, but not so that the universe may circulate. It does not float in blood, it is subject to the order of rhythm. I shall spill my blood so that you will not shed the blood of others. I shall be a joyful source of rhythm and happiness. Thank you, Lord, for letting me flow, for giving me a will that is mine alone, and that now wishes to be a fountain in the night!" And weeping silently, he went bleeding to his hut, followed by his retinue, who also wept.

The people retired to their huts, silent and full of emotion.

Thus ended the third day Quetzalcoatl spent in Tula. And from that day they began to love him.

And thus Quetzalcoatl began his teaching in Anahuac.

A few days later Topiltzin, leading a group of important men, approached Quetzalcoatl, who was teaching his followers how to knit and dye vegetable fibers to make cloth.

"Quetzalcoatl," they said to him, "we have come so that you will talk to us. We want your answers. The people no longer want prisoners to be sacrificed. The priests are angry and have threatened to leave the community. We hesitate and do not know what must be done."

"Very simple," said Quetzalcoatl. "He who accepts the service of God must deal with his own pain and must not cause the pain of others. He who deems it necessary to shed blood must give his own, and must not shed another's. There is no other sacrifice than that of one's own good or of one's own harm. To control another's pain is to steal man's privacy."

"You force us to think, to discern. You destroy the world built by our fathers, the world we have always accepted without discussion. We have believed in the richness of blood as nourishment for the gods, preferably the blood of war prisoners or of heroes. No gift is too great for the gods."

"It is not blood that God asks for. Merit is what he honors. Blood belongs to the generations, and they alone require it. It runs like a flood among men, it passes from fathers to sons. It is thrown into the earth and rots like the hair of the dead. God is no vampire. He nourishes his joy with the merit of men. Merit is what knits the superior light of the spheres."

"And what is this merit of which you speak?"

"To give of one's own, without asking for anything in exchange."

"And what of our own are we to give?"

"Only three things belong to man, and only two are totally pleasing to God: love and pain. Through one, everything is united; through the other, it is separated; and this is the rhythm which makes the universe move. With one, it is bought; with the other, it is paid; and only in this way does the world maintain its balance which is the justice of God. I know it to be so, and so I say it. The third thing is knowledge, but this nourishes arrogance."

"Quetzalcoatl, you say strange things that are beyond our understanding. We do not understand how the pain of man can be pleasing to some god. In truth the god you believe in must be cruel if he rejoices in the pain of his creatures. So far we have only given the gods blood and flowers. We never think of pain."

"Flowers," said Quetzalcoatl, "spring from love. But you have not understood me. Perhaps I do not even understand myself. I am an insignificant dot in the immensity of the earth, and almost nothing in the infinity of the skies. My Lord is not a god of harshness. I have said that the Lord receives merit with pleasure, that merit lies in giving, and

24

that there is nothing more intimate, more attached to the root of man, than his love and his pain."

"Blood or pain," said Topiltzin, "creation seems very strange to me. Now I truly do not understand the world. Why pain? Why?"

"Let us not judge the Creator," Quetzalcoatl said. "Let us answer for our own deeds, that we may live; and let us pray and do penance, that we may know without understanding."

Confused, the men left, saying to each other: "Doubtless, Quetzalcoatl has merit. Now we know less, and yet we no longer want men to be sacrificed."

Then the people met and, after deliberating, decided to have no more sacrifices. "We shall no longer sacrifice men to the gods," they told the priests.

"Foolish!" the priests argued. "Our world will lose its meaning. Another age will come which will not be ours. We do not want to share the fate of Tula. We are going back to the north, to the plains again, to the caves, in search of the essence of this race that is becoming lost. Stay with Quetzalcoatl, he who dances, shouts, and cries. Someday we shall return, or our children shall, to tear out the beard of this demon who has entered the heart of the people!"

And they wrapped the old gods in furs, and headed north with great displeasure. Confusion grew, and many wanted to go with the priests.

But Acatl came, bringing the *teponaxtle,* and Tatle came with a flute that Quetzalcoatl had taught him to make, and the four porters brought rattles and bells, also made by Quetzalcoatl, and they started to beat and to blow into the wood until the music entered the heart of the people once more and confusion vanished.

"Quetzalcoatl gives us beautiful things! Now he has brought the song of birds to the marrow of the swamp reed!"

"Let us go," said the priests, "lest the sound enchant us too, and our decision lose conviction." And, frowning and tight-lipped, they left, dragging their bundles. A few followed them.

"We have been left without gods!" some women cried.

"Quetzalcoatl will create greater ones!" some young men answered. No one was afraid, and they danced until they were exhausted.

The two prisoners took advantage of the dancing and escaped.

On the following day, the leaders again went to Quetzalcoatl, who was again teaching his followers the art of knitting and dyeing vegetable fibers. The work was progressing. And all were surprised at how the weaving created figures in the cloth.

"What surprises you?" asked Quetzalcoatl.

"We came to tell you that we no longer have gods or religion or someone to tell us what is to come and what is to be done, and we have remained here still, watching the magic of your hands and how you form figures with the thread."

"What surprises you?" repeated Quetzalcoatl. "I have already said that all is rhythm and music. The world is like this cloth that I am making. Each one of us goes and comes, and in this way the cloth of creation, with which the Lord adorns himself in his glory, is constructed."

"It will be as you say," said the leaders. "It will be a beautiful cloth."

"Yes," said Quetzalcoatl. "It is a beautiful cloth made of good and bad deeds that only the Lord can see completely. In it the suns of day and night are like precious stones."

And they stayed watching him work and teach.

"We have no gods," they insisted after a while. "Those who left took them. They have hidden them until their return. Give us the new gods whom we are to worship."

"There is only one God," said Quetzalcoatl. "He created the sky and the earth and all things. He is our father and mother. I cannot give him. He is everywhere."

"We cannot see him," they said, "and we cannot understand how he can be one, when everything is different and opposed in this world. Each species has its own protection and is also the enemy of another. The jaguar has large teeth, and the deer great speed in its legs. Some have claws, others horns, others color themselves, many poison. Wherever we look, we see differences. How could there not be a god to take care of each thing? The air, the water, fire, plants, each with their laws and their forms are each taken care of by a different god."

"Do not believe me," said Quetzalcoatl. "God is almighty and, if it were as you say, he would have even created your gods!"

"And who created God?"

"He was not created. The Creation began with time and he does not age. He is identical to himself. He is what is."

"We do not understand," they said. "We need to see, we need to touch. The words you say are not here, they have no

27

bulk. We cannot see them with our eyes, the wind carries them away and we forget them. Give us gods we can understand, who can give pleasure and tranquillity to the people."

"If I am to give you something, I shall plant for you then a cross of arms opened to love and pain. That is the real Tree of the Universe, as was announced by the messengers I sent."

"Give it to us," they said.

"I shall plant it tomorrow. Today I shall carve it."

And he carved with great skill. On the following day the people saw Quetzalcoatl carrying a great cross.

"You will worship this sign. This tree is the truth and the way. The central bough unites the earth and the heavens. One arm is love and the other pain. Accept it as my God, the one who is everywhere and who has all power."

"So will it be," said the people joyfully. "We now have a new god to believe in, the god of Quetzalcoatl.

"We now have one to guide us, to defend us, to sustain us, to give us tranquillity and victory against our enemies. We have a god for our armies.

"We shall adore him. We shall revere him."

They asked, "How shall we please him if blood is no longer permissible?"

"I shall teach you to make beautiful things with stones and precious metals. I shall teach you to make music. I shall teach you to dance and sing. I shall teach you to knit wreaths of flowers and to burn perfumed herbs, and above all, you shall behave as I shall indicate. I shall preach later on. Until then, let faith sustain the tree."

Thus he spoke, and they were all content.

And Quetzalcoatl went to his hut to meditate.

But on the following day, something happened that caused great confusion.

Four of Quetzalcoatl's followers, the ones who had carried him on their shoulders and who loved him greatly, asked for permission to ornament the cross with his image. In order to please him, they devised a serpent of feathers, made with great skill as they had been taught, and wrapped it around the cross so it would look beautiful and not barren.

The people liked it and went to admire it. There were many gathered when Quetzalcoatl arrived. He stepped back and became intensely pale.

"What is it?" he cried. "I do not know him! He is the evil one! He is the arrogant one who drowns my tree! How did he get here?"

"We made him, you allowed it. It is in your likeness. We wanted everyone to know that it was your tree, to know that it was in your care."

"Oh!" Quetzalcoatl moaned. "Now I know I shall not be able to be on the cross. Remove my image! Destroy it with thorns! Let there be no sacrilege. I shall adore the tree with humility, with devotion, but I shall not be able to fasten myself to it. Now I know it. Now I understand. There is too much earth in my body. I am full of arrogance," he said, and was saddened by his vanity.

The people did not understand.

"In truth, he is different from us. We never know how to please him, how to give him satisfaction. We are dull. We are ignorant. We need priests who know about sacred things. We shall ask him to give them to us."

But they did not destroy the serpent. They secretly kept its image in a cave covered with nopal cacti. They began to worship it in secret.

29

For many days he did not go near the cross, nor teach them how to worship it, nor teach religion, nor indoctrinate the people. He was sad, and the people suffered without knowing why.

Then Acatl went to him and said:

"You are sad and quiet. You no longer teach, you no longer speak to us, you do not even meditate. What has angered you? What causes your displeasure? What can the one who sheltered you on the beach do for you? You no longer sing, you have no joy. What shall I do? Shall I pierce my ears and my tongue as little Tatle is doing?"

"What did you say? Have Tatle come!"

They brought Tatle to him, bleeding.

"What are you doing, child?" Quetzalcoatl asked.

"I bring pain upon myself so that happiness may return to your life. So that you will play the flute again. So that you will make nets again. So that you will walk with me again and hold me by the hand. For that I offer my sacrifice."

"This world is mad! I am creating a world of confusion. I have pretended to teach the important things, the great rituals and acts, and I do not even know who I am. There are days when I am full of doubts and confusion, when there is a kind of fog in my spirit. I do not remember what religion is, or the cross, nor do I remember its doctrine, or what steps should be taken next."

"Great has been my vanity and my arrogance. I shall do better if I work with my hands. Hands are humble."

And he told Acatl:

"Beginning today, you will be in charge of the care of the Tree and of its feasts. You will provide the rites. There shall be no blood, but rather songs, flowers, and pleasing smoke instead. Set aside days for feasts and days for atonement and pain. I have taught you for one year. Now you may demonstrate your knowledge."

And he went to the town square to announce it.

"People of Tula!" he shouted with the great voice the people loved to hear. "It will be a man from this earth, the one who is close to me, who rescued me from the sea, dragging me by my beard, who will take care of the Tree I have planted. He will teach religion and the rites. I am not worthy of it because I am arrogant. He is simple, he is well suited. Acatl will take care of the Tree and say how it is to be worshipped. I shall travel over the land. I want to begin to know it. I want to teach things useful for the soil. I do not want to create more confusion in your souls. I want to meditate. I want to remember, lest I lead you astray."

The people accepted Quetzalcoatl's decision. They needed someone to take charge of the sacred things so that order and contentment would return with the joy, the dancing, and the songs of the first days.

In this way Quetzalcoatl decided to get to know the land in which he was to live for fifty-two years. He left with his followers, and he asked Topiltzin to accompany him.

"I shall prepare you to rule over the good things for the body that I shall teach. Come," he said to him. "Come with me. Choose the people who will accompany you and who know the region."

Topiltzin was happy because he had a curious spirit and was always asking about things.

But it did not seem right to everyone that Quetzalcoatl should appoint someone to rule over the rites and someone to rule over the things of the body. Envy began to grow in some, but still it was kept hidden.

Quetzalcoatl went out in a feathered cloak and with a great crest on his head. He gave his hand to Tatle, who

31

went along joyfully, realizing he had not tortured himself in vain.

He walked through the region closely observing the land, looking for places where he could sow corn with the best results. He scouted for fields to grow cotton, chili, pumpkins, and the other fruits of the land. He looked for places where water could be dammed, where there was stone to carve and build with, where there were metals and precious stones, where there was game. He found them all and other things too.

Quetzalcoatl drew it all on the thin skins he pulled from century plants and bark. The people were surprised that lines could be drawn using thorns from the century plant and oils and juices from other plants.

"You are skillful in many arts, Quetzalcoatl."

"I shall teach them all. The people will be skillful and rich. They will be builders, they will be craftsmen, they will be called the Toltecs."

One day he and his followers went to some distant mountains, and Topiltzin said to him:

"We will not be able to go beyond here without fighting. The land of the savage Chichimecs begins here. They are strong fighters who do not settle in villages. They go from place to place in search of the wild animals which they eat."

"I shall take my message to them. But it will be later on, when our land has grown."

"It will be difficult," replied Topiltzin. "They hardly speak, they understand nothing beyond their simple things, and they have no contact with strangers. They have no chiefs, no one rules over them, they worship the sun and the stars, but without priests to organize them. Their lives are brief and brutish. They are simple, like arrows."

"If that is the way they are, they will understand me well!

We shall come some day, but now it is time to go back to Tula. I want to see how Acatl has been taking care of the Tree."

And they returned with samples and drawings of the things of the land. The trip had lasted three months.

From the distance, between the hills, they saw the houses of Tula.

"We shall soon build a new Tula, which will be the pride of the land. It will be made of carved stone and beautiful colors pleasing to the eye."

Acatl went to greet him with great joy.

"It has been done as you ordered. The people have accepted this new god, and we have marked the days when we will dance and sing for him. We already have four *teponaxtles,* four flutes, and many bells and tambourines. Those who will play them have already been appointed according to the ability they have demonstrated. I have already appointed someone to keep the square clean. However, we have not worshipped the Tree, nor do we know how, or what to speak to it about. It has no human likeness, nor does it represent anything we know. You will have to teach us. And I must tell you something else: more and more people are going to a cave where they say the plumed serpent is kept. They say it is your twin, the one who gives you strength, because the Tree deprives you of your precious blood. They tell me that, in order to augment your power, they have begun to sacrifice to it—doves, birds, animals that fly—and they say it will give you strength to continue your work for the good of the people. What are we to do?"

"Go to that cave," Quetzalcoatl told him. "See what it is all about, what their cult is, and if they do evil things."

And Acatl did so.

He went at night, when the people were asleep and

would not know. He arrived as the reddish moon hung over the place where the sun had set. He entered the cave without being seen by the four porters, the ones who had made the serpent and who were now worshipping it. They had just sacrificed a dove whose blood was still sputtering on the embers with the smouldering copal. A dense and perfumed smoke filled the cave and made the senses whirl. They were seated, moving rhythmically, while they pierced their ears and passed string through their tongues. The light of the embers turned everything red. The serpent seemed to move. They were singing something in a low murmur. They had given the serpent obsidian eyes, and it seemed to be looking at everyone. The eyes shone as if they were its own, as if they were alive.

Acatl could not keep his eyes from the serpent. The smoke of the copal and the smell of the burnt blood flooded his senses. The rhythm of the song began to possess his body and he prostrated himself. He started to murmur the prayer.

The porters watched him for a long while, without interrupting what they were doing. Acatl extended his hands and they gave him needles and ropes with which he too tortured himself.

"In truth he is the precious twin," Acatl whispered. "He will unite us all. He will make Quetzalcoatl strong so that he can make us strong and pure. He is his image, he is like the echo of his mother who looked for him in the heavens while I looked for him on the earth and in the sea."

"Yes," the porters said, "this is the image we understand. The other one is bare and dry. It is a withered and sad tree, it has no colors and it resembles nothing. This is the twin image of Quetzalcoatl. It is what he wants without knowing it, what he will know when the fog in his mind has cleared, when he remembers his world and his origins, when he remembers the mother you have seen."

"We shall worship it here without his knowledge until the day comes when it shall be enthroned in his temple. We shall nourish our devotion here," Acatl concluded. "During the day I shall clean the cross and attend to the stipulated rites. During the night I shall come here with you, here where the real god of Quetzalcoatl lives, the one who is his twin and who will take him to the heavens. He ordered us to do it for the good of the land. Let us give thanks!"

On the following day he went to Quetzalcoatl and told him:

"I have gone as you ordered. The serpent is lying in a corner. It is dirty and drying up. No one is there to see it. The people only go to the cave to protect themselves from the rain."

"If that is the way it is," said Quetzalcoatl, "there is no reason why it should be dirty. See to it that it does not dry up. I see no harm in setting it apart. The feathers are beautiful and they have covered me many times."

In this way, without realizing, Quetzalcoatl began to feel the temptation to become a god.

CHAPTER III

❦

The Toltecs,
the Builders

AT THAT TIME, Quetzalcoatl was entering the prime of his life. He was tall and his limbs were strong. He was beautiful. He liked to go out in his brilliantly feathered capes and crests to be admired by the people. They loved him because he was different and did great good.

He had organized them according to their abilities and they were happy. Truly a new age was beginning.

He had separated those who tilled the soil from those who were to work in the city.

He taught them the usefulness of common effort, and how to divide labor and the gifts of life.

He taught them to cultivate the land so that it would yield rich crops, to store water, and to conduct it along canals to the places where it was needed.

He taught them to grow cotton, to harvest it, and to twist it to make thread. He taught them to fish and to catch birds with nets and traps.

He taught them to carve wood.

He taught them to soften furs, and how to make dyes from small shells, earth, oils, and animals.

He taught them how to weave bright-colored blankets.

He taught them how to gather gold from the rivers, and how to separate it from the sand; to extract metals from the earth, to purify them, melt them, and make them into jewelry.

He taught them how to find precious stones, to polish and arrange them so that they would glitter and shine.

He taught them how to build great houses, with every detail planned.

He told them, "You will be the Toltecs, the builders, the artisans. Your fame will spread throughout the land, and soon the entire Anahuac will come to admire and to learn. You must learn that there are two ways to please God: by giving him the merit of our suffering and by receiving his gifts with humility and work. At first I spoke to you of death. Now I want to teach you to live, to sow, and to harvest so that we may all thank the goodness of God."

For a long time he had not gone near the square where the Tree of the Universe was planted. Acatl was still taking care of it and, although rites were still being performed, more and more people were going to worship the serpent in the cave, taking it rich offerings.

Quetzalcoatl had neither the time nor the desire to ask about it. He seldom spoke with Acatl, who was becoming more devoted to the cult of the serpent. He was happy because he was increasing the strength and wisdom of Quetzalcoatl and the prosperity and beauty of Tula. Acatl was content. He had found meaning in his life.

Tatle was growing up by Quetzalcoatl's side. "You are

my son, as though you were of my own blood," he would say to him. "I shall give you my wisdom and all my power. You will make this land grow."

Tatle was a silent and withdrawn child. He learned everything with unusual speed and hardly spoke to anyone. He watched and admired Quetzalcoatl.

"You will be as I would like to be," Quetzalcoatl often told him. And he made him lead an austere life.

"I shall be as you want," Tatle would answer. But he was not happy. He knew that Quetzalcoatl was enveloped in a mist.

Quetzalcoatl had begun to like wearing jewelry. He ornamented himself with gold and emeralds, and would go out for the people to admire him. They liked to see him covered with precious feathers, gold, and stones. And they loved him more and more.

It was then that he decided to build a house with many great rooms.

"I shall build this house for the heart of the people. In it we shall keep its things. This is where my retinue, the servants of the people, will live. Here I shall teach more things."

They took a long time to build the house, which was round in the center and had four great wings spreading out toward the four cardinal points. They built storehouses for the rich harvests that had been reaped, as there was no space left for them.

The great house went up as the richness and power of Tula grew. It was all made of carved stones and it had flat roofs. Quetzalcoatl had building materials sent from all the corners of the region. He worked without haste, choosing four beautiful colors for the stones and ornaments.

The people admired this and took delight in working on the great mansion, which rose on a hill so that it could be seen from anyplace in Tula.

The Toltecs—as they were now called—began to know great abundance and enjoy the generous gifts of the land, as had been foretold by Quetzalcoatl.

"He has great powers. He has made us rich. We have not known hunger since he arrived. Where he places his eyes and hands, everything is abundance and beauty."

They were happy, they were proud. At that time they all still worked at the jobs Quetzalcoatl assigned to them.

Tula grew. People came from afar to admire its growth. Many asked permission to settle down and enjoy its abundance, which was distributed according to the needs of the people. Topiltzin was in charge of distributing the riches, under the orders of Quetzalcoatl, so that no one would want. They were all content because they all had more than they had ever had. Many worked. They were busy all day.

Quetzalcoatl had spent six years among the Toltecs. The house for the heart of the people was almost finished and the granaries full when he decided:

"There is prosperity and abundance in all the land. Let us extend it beyond the mountains. We shall go to the land of the Chichimecs. It is time to take my mission to them. I shall make them better, I shall make them live together, I shall gather them in towns, I shall teach them to till the land and to build their homes."

"Let us leave them in their land as they are now," Topiltzin argued. "They are barbarous, their life is violent and disorderly. They roam freely, like the wind in the mountains and the plains, with nothing to keep them, nothing to retain them. Leave them where they are. There is much that we must do in our own land."

"I do not belong to this land alone. They are all my brothers, and I am to give to all of them. I shall look for them. I shall take the gods of Tula to them," Quetzalcoatl said.

"Think carefully about what we shall do. You do not know them. They do not understand words. They are like savage animals, like jaguars," Topiltzin insisted.

"I shall go," said Quetzalcoatl. "My life must be accomplished. This time you will not accompany me because you do not have the will to go. I shall leave soon with some of my followers."

"Do not go with so few people! I shall accompany you with skillful warriors who are used to killing Chichimecs and avoiding their traps," Topiltzin insisted.

"I am not going there with violence. I shall go to them as I came here, to take them the gifts of life and the doctrine of sin and redemption."

"You have not spoken of sin and redemption for a long time," Tatle remarked. He had been listening intently to the dialogue, and was then close to seventeen years of age. "You have not come near the Tree you planted in the square in a long time. The Tree has no shoots, it has not grown, it looks sad and lonely."

"During this time, Tatle, I have often thought of it. There was confusion in my spirit. Now the Tree orders me to spread good in other lands, to make other brothers happy. It will soon have shoots."

"The Chichimecs are not our brothers!" cried Topiltzin. "They have been in this land for a long time. They are strange and ferocious. They eat everything, even garbage. They only worship the sun and the arrow. They like to kill and they die young. Do not leave us; there are people here who look up to you and accept the gifts you bring and

41

teach. You want to go to where you're not wanted and will not be received."

"I will go. It is not good to remain still when there is so much to be done."

And he called Acatl to prepare for the trip.

Acatl had gained great dignity. The people respected him because he was in charge of the cult and the rites; he was the one who had rescued Quetzalcoatl, and who, with the four porters, had founded and extended the cult of the plumed serpent, the precious twin who inspired all of Quetzalcoatl's deeds without his knowledge.

He wore cloaks similar to the one Quetzalcoatl first made. He ornamented his lips and ears with gold plates in which he inserted feathers, so that it looked as if he had a multicolored beard. He walked solemnly and said little. When he arrived, he said:

"You have called me, my lord. I have news that you want to leave us to look for the world of the Chichimecs. You want to make them better."

"So will it be," said Quetzalcoatl. "I have called you to dig up the Tree in the square. It will be carried by the four porters who carried me on my arrival in Tula, and they will accompany me to the land of the Chichimecs. *Teponaxtle* and flute players are to come with me. They must come with bells and tambourines."

"Take Topiltzin and the warriors," Acatl suggested.

"I shall not take violence where there is violence. I shall take the Tree of Life and the way. I shall take the harmony of wood. I need nothing else."

"It will be done as you say. May we not live to regret it!"

"And one more thing I say to you," Quetzalcoatl added. "See to it that the cult of the serpent is no longer practiced as I know is now being done, or I shall return to destroy it with my own hands!"

Acatl said nothing, but his eyes were filled with tears.

Early on the following day Quetzalcoatl left with a small group of followers, including Tatle. The four porters carried the cross. No warriors accompanied the group, only musicians and artisans.

Topiltzin secretly followed Quetzalcoatl with a group of strong warriors.

For many days Quetzalcoatl walked until he arrived at the land of the Chichimecs and wandered through it without seeing a soul. The people began to feel weary and said:

"Quetzalcoatl, these savages want nothing from us. They flee like the wind, they vanish like the air. From a distance, we think we see them; up close, we sense them, but they never face us."

Then Quetzalcoatl decided to stop wandering. He settled in a valley and said:

"We shall make a great fire for many nights. Around it we shall play our wooden instruments. We shall fix the cross in the center until the hidden ones come to us. They will come in search of light and harmony, and light and harmony I will give to their lives."

For three nights they did this and nothing happened. The fire could be seen from afar, and music echoed from the mountain rocks. The only responses were the howls of coyotes and the roar of jaguars.

From a distance, Topiltzin kept guard.

But on the fourth night, when no one expected them, they arrived silently. They were many. They were naked, armed with stones, sticks, and arrows. The night had been terrifying, full of cries and howls.

The first to see them, just at the limit of the fire's light, was Tatle. He sat up slowly. He could vaguely see their bodies, the gleam of their eyes like obsidian, their long straight hair hanging in dirty strands.

"There they are! They have come!" called Tatle, and everything became still, except for the bonfire and the howls of the coyotes.

"At a good time," Quetzalcoatl said. And just as he sat up, Tatle was struck with the first arrow.

"No! No! No!" Quetzalcoatl cried. The savages answered with a great hissing, and they imitated him, "No! No! No!", while a shower of stones fell on the helpless group.

"Weapons! We need weapons!" cried some of the men.

"Do not resist!" he called to them. "I won't fall again to the temptation of violence! Play *teponaxtles* and flutes! I will speak!"

He opened his cloak with his great arms and cried "Chichimecs, brothers!", and a stone hit him in the mouth and arrows struck his body. He fell heavily over Tatle.

"Cover the cross!" he managed to cry while again the night of madness came.

The porters rushed to cover Quetzalcoatl's body, and they were killed with stones and arrows.

There was great confusion. Many ran into the dark night and fell into the hands of the Chichimecs and were beaten to death. Others remained still, praying to their old gods, and were also killed.

The screams of the savage Chichimecs bounced like arrows on the sides of the mountains.

They danced until they broke the *teponaxtles* and threw them into the fire. They smashed the flutes into splinters, screaming and laughing.

They were demolishing the cross when, covered with

blood, Quetzalcoatl tried to sit up and murmured something that could not be heard. A new arrow pierced his body and again he fell. Five flint-tipped arrows were embedded in his sides and legs. From a distance, the harsh and desperate cry of combat could be heard by Topiltzin's warriors, who could not advance quickly in the darkness of the night.

The Chichimecs ceased their uproar and scattered in groups, one of which took Quetzalcoatl while the others took several dead or wounded men. They were taking them to their women and children in order to eat them together. When Topiltzin's warriors arrived, the bonfire was still burning. Tatle had regained consciousness and, sobbing, said:

"They have taken him! They are taking him! They are taking my Father! They are leaving me without light! They are leaving me without faith! They are leaving me alone in this world of violence! Truly the evil one has been set loose tonight! They have destroyed the Tree, they have struck us with arrows!"

It took the warriors three days and three nights to recover the wounded body of Quetzalcoatl. Gloomy and desperate, they followed the tracks into the mountains. When they finally caught up, the meeting was brief and cruel. The ten Chichimecs, exhausted from carrying the body, were murdered on the spot.

Once again Quetzalcoatl's body was lying on the ground, his stomach pressed to the earth. The remaining feathers of his cloak only covered part of his body, stuck to him by his dried blood. From a distance, he once again looked like a plumed serpent.

Exhausted, panting, full of the horror and the violence of combat, they fell on their knees when they realized Quetzalcoatl was still alive. They made a bed of sticks and blankets and began the descent, watching him with care, washing and dressing his wounds. They removed the arrowheads embedded in his flesh, but he did not regain consciousness. They gave him water and honey.

One night, while they were resting, Quetzalcoatl tried to sit up and began talking and singing in a strange and remote language. They all listened anxiously and said:

"He cannot die! He will come back to us! He will continue to make Tula great and strong! He must be calling his mother. He must be calling her in her own language." And they listened, absorbed and compassionate.

Later they came to the place where the bonfire had been. Quetzalcoatl was very weak. Fever had turned his wasted face red. Topiltzin wept and said:

"This is where you fell, Quetzalcoatl, without defending yourself! We warned you! The Chichimecs are as simple as wind and arrows. They understand nothing, they are interested in nothing. You can say nothing to those who do not understand you. You can give nothing to those who need nothing but the freedom to wander. I told you!" and he fell on his knees in desperation.

They hastened their march. People from Tula now came with reinforcements. The terrible news had reached them, but no one wanted to believe it.

"The savage Chichimecs have destroyed Quetzalcoatl. They are taking him to eat him and make their hearts bigger. They want to steal our Quetzalcoatl."

The people were weeping in the streets and in the square.

"They have taken our Quetzalcoatl. We will be alone again, scattered in the middle of the land, crying like children!

"We shall be alone in the middle of the land!

"We shall be alone in the middle of the land!

"We shall be alone, crying like children!

"We shall be alone!"

Serene, dignified, majestic, Acatl came to the square with open arms. He was wearing his great feathered cloak, and his feathered beard quivered and gleamed in the afternoon.

"Brother Toltecs!" he cried. "Quetzalcoatl shall not die! He shall only leave us when he wills it, and not while there is a will that he remain alive. He survived the night and the storm and he does not want to die. He has said it to me many times. He shall not die! But we must give him strength. Now he has a people who will help him return from darkness. We shall bring the serpent out of the cave and enthrone it in the empty square. We shall worship it there; we shall sing, dance and sing to please it. We shall offer sacrifices so that it may give strength to its suffering twin. We shall give it our own blood, the blood of the people's heart. Quetzalcoatl shall not die!"

The people became calm. Some went for the serpent, some for Quetzalcoatl.

They carried him in shifts and never stopped walking, day or night. He arrived in Tula stretched out and unconscious. With him was the half-burned cross he had taken.

All the people received him and took him to the house of the heart of the people, to a great unfinished room which they prepared with blankets and feathers. There he was left to rest.

His body was bundled. Acatl and the shamans surrounded and washed him, dressed his wounds and watched over him through the night, invoking the powers of health. Yet they saw no improvement.

On the following day Acatl addressed the people from the roof, saying:

47

"He has arrived alive, and he will remain alive. But it is time to enthrone his twin, to obtain his salvation. It is time to take the serpent out of the cave and render it to the sun. It is time to go up to the pyramid and to build him a taller and more beautiful one in the way he has taught us. We must carve stones with the signs of the plumed serpent and paint them with pleasing colors. Let us prepare the land. Have the people make a road from the cave to the temple with their own blood and, with it, have them sprinkle the place where he will rest. It will be a voluntary sacrifice. The sacrifice of those who love Quetzalcoatl.

"Quetzalcoatl needs our sacrifice!

"Let us redeem his suffering with ours!

"Let us give life to his death!

"Let us give blood to the twin!

"We shall not remain alone in the middle of the earth!

"He will be like a father to us again!

"He will walk by our side again!

"We shall not fall back into darkness!

"He will go on as our light, our truth, our way!

"In this way we shall raise our prayer to the precious twin!

"He will make him return!

"Let us give to him and implore him!

"Each one should do as he has to do!"

The people prepared the way as Acatl instructed. It was sprinkled with blood and tears. Blood and tears prepared the serpent's bed.

At dawn on the following day they took the serpent out of the cave. The song of the *teponaxtle,* the whistling of the reeds, and the hoarse sound of the shell they brought from the sea, all flooded the air with a persevering obsession. Not once did the sound cease as they carried the serpent, wrapped around the Tree of Life, up to the pinnacle of what was then the pyramid of Tula. Acatl led them, carrying the serpent's head. He was wearing gold sandals and Quetzalcoatl's robes and jewels.

The serpent was left, coiled, at the top of the temple. The round eyes of obsidian shone mysteriously. Acatl himself had arranged the feathers, and it looked magnificent. The ceremony lasted till sunset. Then Acatl ordered the people to go back to Quetzalcoatl's house and to pray in whispers for the life of the one who was like their father, and to watch over him all night. They did so.

Acatl stayed behind to sacrifice his own blood to the serpent. He cried for the pain of his four companions who could not join him in his sorrow. They had been his friends, the silent ones, the ones who never complained. Acatl missed them, prayed for their health, asked for their blessing.

In this way he spent half the night. He went into a state of ecstasy. He became detached from the world. He was the serpent, he was Quetzalcoatl, he was the father and the mother. He was the whole universe reverted to its original navel. The constellations of sun and light slowly turned around him and he was suspended, weightless and unconscious, in the center of all things. He did not know if time was going by. An instant or an eternity passed.

Suddenly the constellations turned into words of light that called his name.

"Acatl! Acatl!" It was the quiet, respectful voice of Tatle, who was impressed by the martyr's transformed face, upturned eyes, and bleeding, half-opened mouth. "Do something! Our Quetzalcoatl is dying! He awoke and did not recognize us. He said many words in a strange language that no one understood, and then he cried, 'God! God! Man! The People!' and then he seemed to be dead."

"I shall go," Acatl said in a distant, low voice. "Once more I shall rescue him from the shore. Once more I shall drag him by his beard and hair. I shall feed him again. I shall make a gift of him to this land. I will do it! I will do it! I have seen! I have seen! I shall go for him to the navel of the universe. I shall go for him to the wind and darkness. From there I shall drag him to the earth, to this other half of the world, with my hands and with my blood. My time has come. I have come to my time. It is the hour that was not! I am going!"

And he staggered up as if he were walking in his sleep. And all the people who had come for him were amazed and said, "He has entered the serpent's spirit! He has been transformed!" and they opened a path for him in silence, with downcast eyes.

When he arrived at the square, he spoke again:

"I want a great fire here. A greater fire than Tula has ever seen. You will do this, and when I depart you will build a new pyramid on top of the old one, and that will be the great house of the serpent."

And he walked slowly and with hesitation to Quetzalcoatl's house.

He found him lying on a mat as if dead. He had thrown the blankets from himself and was naked, unconscious.

"Brother, little brother," Acatl said to him, "I am going for you! I know the way! You have taught me the way of the universe, the path that runs between the two halves. You have taught me the way that man can follow. I shall go back to Omeyocan. There I shall be myself, the one I am and the one I shall no longer be. From there you shall come back to

Tula, to the ones you love, to the ones who love you, to the ones who receive your good and your gifts. From there I shall carry you. I shall go quickly, along the shortest route."

He said all this and then kissed Quetzalcoatl's beard. He was silent for a long time, squatting, until they came to tell him that a great fire was burning in the square, a fire greater than had ever been seen before. It looked like the rising sun.

"It is time. It is my time. I shall go. I am going."

He walked with a steady pace. He climbed to the top of the pyramid, and he spoke from there. Some were able to hear his words.

"I am Ce-Acatl," he told them. "I am the first man of the new age. I am the first fastening. Let me not be the last. I shall soon be on my way to the shore, to bring from the sea, from the wind, from darkness, the spirit of Quetzalcoatl that wanders between mist and oblivion. I am going to Omeyocan, to the Second Place, where everything exists and perishes at the same time. I am going with the firm will of a perishable man, to build my own universe from the two halves. It will be made of light and love. Someday it will be established on this earth. He has announced it from his mist, from his oblivion, and with all the strength of his good will. I am going with mine, which makes me similar to him. I shall be his twin. I shall make myself his twin, his equal. I am a spark in the immensity of the stars. I shall be the morning star. I know what I am. I know where I am going."

He took the plumed serpent, wrapped it around his arms and back and, without uttering a sound, walked slowly down the steps and into the fire. His body flared for a moment and then burst into a great spark that rose to the sky.

"His heart has risen," the people prayed, "and silence has been created!"

At dawn the next day, before the fire had gone out, a strong rain fell and extinguished the embers. It did not stop raining for three days.

And as it rained, Quetzalcoatl regained his senses and began his recovery.

❧

Ce-Acatl

ACATL! ACATL! BROTHER!" were the first words he was able to speak. "You have given me water and honey again! Acatl! Acatl!"

But Acatl did not come. He called Acatl throughout the first day of rain and Acatl did not come.

On the second day of rain, Tatle went to him: "Father Quetzalcoatl. It is useless for you to call Ce-Acatl. He has already left for Omeyocan. He entered the fire willingly and his heart flew up to the sky. Now I think he returns in water, in rain. It has rained without stopping for two days since the water put out the bonfire through which he left. He departed for the bank of the two halves. He went for you and now you are among us again. He left with the serpent. He said he was your twin."

"God! God!" Quetzalcoatl cried. And he said nothing more that day. He closed his eyes and slept for a long while.

On the third day, he called Tatle.

"Son. Now you are the youngest and the oldest. You will not abandon me; you will accompany me until I finish my passage through this land. You will help me be the one I am because your eyes understand me better than my own do.

"Call the people, have them all come out in the rain, let them all come simply dressed. They will witness my taking a new name by which I shall also be known."

Tatle asked Topiltzin, who had been sad and somber, to call the people to gather in front of the house where Quetzalcoatl lived. They came in the rain, excited and curious. "Our Quetzalcoatl is reuniting us again. Ce-Acatl has brought him back to us."

Simply dressed in a white tunic, Quetzalcoatl went out on the flat roof. He was leaning on Tatle and Topiltzin. It was raining in torrents. "Toltecs!" he said weakly. And they all missed his old voice. They had to repeat his words among themselves so that they could hear him through the rain and thunder.

"You will witness a new name I want to take and by which you shall also know me. I have been reborn here twice! Each time I become more a part of this land! I shall receive my name from the water that falls from the sky and from the beginning of my time! I shall be called Ce-Acatl. First Cane, first fastening of this land! It is the name of my twin, with whom I am as one. The one who has twice brought me from the bank and who now lives in my heart. It is the name of the one who left through fire and returns through water. It is the name of my brother, of my twin. I shall also be called Ce-Acatl. A cane that becomes a serpent at the beginning of time. He left because he wanted my life, and now I am reborn anew. I take the name from water which washes all filth. I receive it from my breast where now two hearts, two twin halves beat. I receive it from the Lord who is in the heavens. I shall love this land with these two hearts. Go in the rain, Toltecs, and from now on and forever you will also call me Ce-Acatl."

They went away joyfully at having Quetzalcoatl, who in his heart had Ce-Acatl, among them again.

A few days later, Quetzalcoatl spoke with Tatle in this way:

"Son, the first thing I shall do when I recover my strength will be to build the great pyramid that Ce-Acatl wanted. We shall dedicate it to him. It will be high and beautiful; the plumed serpent will be wrapped around all its terraces; we shall paint it in four colors and it will merit his suffering."

"It will doubtless be beautiful," remarked Tatle, who had a profound spirit in spite of his young age. He said:

"Quetzalcoatl, you are like my father. Since I found you lying on the beach and poked your body a long time ago, you have taken over my will, and I have followed you—and will follow you—as you say until you leave this land. I am nearly a man now, and already the world pains me. I suffer from everything and I have questions and want answers. I have seen Acatl transfigured. He was no longer in this world when he went to the pyramid to ask it to do something for you. I saw him enter the fire without hesitating, as if it were a feast. My hair still stands on end. I asked myself, and ask myself now, is it necessary? Is this earth, full of sorrow and bitterness, necessary? Does it purchase anything? That stupid and burning pain that is found without asking, that comes like an arrow when one tries to escape from it, that stupid pain that kills and devours and makes one hate the life on which it feeds—is it necessary, lord? Is it like coin which compensates for everything in this nook where we dwell? Does that pain go up, like copal smoke, making the gods drunk? Why, lord, why? I saw him suffer and burn and become transformed. What for?"

"Hush, Tatle, be silent! You say things in your youth

that I do not dare think about. I have no answer; I lack the coin with which to pay for your question. I can only offer you the pain caused by having no answer. I do not know, Tatle! I do not know! Once before, the old men asked me the same question and I was not able to remain silent. Now it is your youth that asks, and it is the death of our Acatl and my ignorance that answer: I do not know, Tatle! A mist envelops me: I only know I accept my destiny; I only know that I am not to deny the order of God's will; I only know I love him and affirm him; that I answer nothing and love everything; that my will accepts pain in the same way as it loves God. Think no more; do not torture yourself with questions. Silence as an answer is a deep, black, boundless suffering."

"You say terrible things to me, Quetzalcoatl! It seems as though suffering, thinking, and loving were all the same thing, a horrible, deep, black, boundless suffering. What is the limit? If you cannot answer me, then who has the answer? Where shall I go to find it? What shall I have to pay to have it answered?"

"Tatle, I am sure Acatl has found the answer. He filled his heart with love and his will with giving."

"But he is not here to answer me."

"You want to know, Tatle; he only wanted to get there and he has already left."

"Oh, Father Quetzalcoatl! Now I am invaded by a great desire to cry, to cry for everything! I would like to burst into pieces and have every piece go off in search of an answer that would later be sung in every sphere. Everything pains me, Quetzalcoatl! The world pains me. God pains me."

"You suffer, Tatle, weep! I shall weep with you, my son!"

CHAPTER V

❦

The Pyramid

QUETZALCOATL recovered but had not begun the building of the great pyramid that Acatl wanted. For a year he only studied with the wise men the rotation of the stars.

Then Topiltzin, leading the most important men, went to see him and said:

"Quetzalcoatl, the people are anxious to build the great pyramid for the serpent—a pyramid as has never been seen in this land— and we want to build it according to your instructions."

"I have already devised it, Topiltzin; it will face the four points and be subject to the days and years. Now I am studying the skies, together with the wisest of the Toltecs; we are putting together all we know so that the plan will be complete.

"However, I cannot make up my mind because it would be an undertaking requiring many years and an effort as great as the light of the fire that devoured Acatl."

"It will be an undertaking worthy of the Toltecs," Topiltzin remarked.

"Yes," Quetzalcoatl replied. "But we would be exhausted; we would lack sufficient numbers of men. I have thought of making it with enormous, engraved stones. But dragging them would exhaust us. There are few Toltecs who would be able to work on this. They all work in the land or in the city, at jobs that could not be abandoned because what used to be ignorance has now become necessity."

"The people want to build it, Quetzalcoatl. We would strive for it!"

"It would exhaust us, Topiltzin, because only a pyramid worthy of Acatl's greatness should be built."

"And of the great power of the serpent," concluded Topiltzin, who also added, "I shall confer with the people."

On the following day he went back to Quetzalcoatl and told him:

"The people will build the pyramid you have devised. We shall work hard from dawn to dusk. We want to honor the memory of Ce-Acatl and give tribute to the precious twin."

"May it so be!" said Quetzalcoatl, "and may we not regret it later on."

It was in this way that, exactly a year after Acatl's death, they began the construction of the great pyramid for the precious twin. It volume grew as did the richness and power of Tula. Its prestige spread throughout the land of Anahuac. The various regions received and accepted Tula's influence.

It was then that the Toltecs began to abandon the more menial jobs and to entrust them to other men. The great stones were moved on wooden rollers along the roads that led to Tula. From distant places men carried on their backs the materials with which Tula's greatness was being built. And there were other people who dragged, pushed, and endured.

But the work did not progress with enough speed.

"We need more men for the heavy work. The Toltecs no longer accept unskilled work and we need someone to do it," Quetzalcoatl pointed out.

"We shall have to bring people from far away," Topiltzin said. "I have been thinking about it for a long time. Let us teach the power of Tula to all the inhabitants of Anahuac. Let us attract them with our wealth. Let us take our commerce to them and tempt them with our diverse arts."

In this way many were attracted, and they willingly accepted work in Tula, where they served.

"Another pyramid is being built in Tula," Tatle remarked one day. "The outsiders are giving us a base. It is difficult to find familiar faces; I can no longer find the original equality among so many strange and different people whom it is hard to love as brothers, as you order, Quetzalcoatl."

"I see, Tatle, and I think that, as with the pyramid, we must form and order this great crowd to avoid chaos."

But at the time Quetzalcoatl was more interested in the paths of the stars and the problem was neglected.

Later on a great lack of men to drag the stones coincided with the return of a commercial expedition sent by Topiltzin to the land of the Chichimecs. Few came back. They had been assaulted, robbed, and killed. The savage men neither understood nor wanted commerce. The Toltecs were indignant at the repeated arrogance of the Chichimecs. Topiltzin met with Quetzalcoatl.

"Your way will not be concluded unless you take your work to the land of the Chichimecs. Their elementary brutality checks our commerce. They know nothing; they neither give nor ask. They are absurd people who are possessed by demons and they hinder Tula's expansion."

"They did not want to hear me," observed Quetzalcoatl. "They do not even know how to hear."

"Let us teach them how!" said Topiltzin. "It is time they learned your message, which is now the truth of the Toltecs; it is time they worshipped and gave tribute to the precious twin; it is time they became aware of their savagery, and that we can bring them out of it. It is time they stopped killing so that harmony, the shadow of your Tree, can reign among them."

"I wonder," Quetzalcoatl replied, "if it is fair or possible to convince them by force, as it would be difficult to persuade them by any other means."

"It is our duty," Topiltzin retorted. "We are above and we must teach those who do not understand. The entire Anahuac must contemplate the majesty of the twin, contribute to it, and increase Tula's greatness."

"It is hard to admit that harmony should be imposed by means of violence," Quetzalcoatl contended.

"But think," Topiltzin insisted, "that force only gives in to force and that reason is helpless when there is no willingness to listen to it. You once wanted to go with only your voice, and they broke your mouth, as they broke the song of the wood, as they smashed the flutes to splinters, and killed our companions, and as they now have destroyed our commercial expedition. They will remain as they are unless a firm hand stops this race of savage buffalo and settles them in the land so that they become true men and appreciate the gift of life, so that their lives are no longer the brief, brutish, fleeting transit which they now live."

"But," Quetzalcoatl objected weakly, "they need nothing of what we can give them."

"We needed nothing before you came, and now we would not be able to live without it."

"But you accepted it," said Quetzalcoatl.

"We shall have to teach them to accept it. It is our duty. You have taught us the duty of giving and teaching."

It was in this way that, tempted by Topiltzin, Quetzalcoatl consented to the conquest of the Chichimecs, who succumbed to Toltec strength and were dragged into serving in the construction of the pyramid and into the life of Tula.

"You went to meekly serve them," said the proud Topiltzin, who had become very powerful while he headed the armies of the Toltecs. "But they only accepted violence. This time we went like a stormy wind and now they are tame. We improve them and teach them how to build the pyramids."

Quetzalcoatl was confused and Tatle realized it. But the pyramid was going up quickly and Quetzalcoatl continued studying the skies.

One day Quetzalcoatl himself heard the cries of the carriers who fell under the whip, and he tore his eyes away from the stars and walked with Tatle, who was nearly a man then, along the roads that led to Tula, through the districts inhabited by the newcomers and the huts in which the Chichimec prisoners lived.

"Now the people die of exhaustion and need," Tatle remarked. "They suffer and I do not think they know why."

"Yes," Quetzalcoatl agreed. "Our pyramid has grown greatly and those who are beneath are dying, crushed by its great weight. There must be a remedy."

And he went to look for Topiltzin. He found him surrounded by a retinue of important warriors and told him:

"Topiltzin! Help me find a remedy! I have witnessed the death of many men who come from far away and I have seen others in great need."

"Yes," said Topiltzin. "It is the price that has to be paid to build the pyramid! It should not be the Toltecs who die crushed by the great weight! We are already above; we have risen from the dust in which they now lie!"

"May the dust not prevent us from seeing!" Quetzalcoatl exclaimed. "There is no use in a pyramid if it is only a heap, if there is nothing in it with harmony and good intention. The mountains will always be higher, and yet on their peaks the creator is not worshipped. We want to enthrone the twin at a great height that has been achieved through our own effort, in which each stone is touched by the hand of man and his good intention."

"But, Quetzalcoatl, those are merely beautiful words! You are always saying them to the young Tatle. You and he are always thinking and saying beautiful things. I have been charged with moving the men, and it has not been my encouragement but my fists that have achieved it. A great crowd, Quetzalcoatl, is like a great flood with which one tries to exchange words in vain. It is necessary to mark its course and it will dash against it until it runs in a soft and orderly way. You are the one who told me where you want to go and I have been the one who led the way. Some have died; and, doubtless, still more will die. Many suffer. We have suffered. You yourself have. It is the law that rules over everything."

"I am not afraid of pain, Topiltzin; I am hurt by injustice. These people used to be apart from us, and now they suffer on our account. We do not do them justice; we do not give them what they need. We take from them all they can give us."

"But you have spent a long time studying the stars and measuring the periods of their rotation with your threads. For a long time we have not lived in the simplicity of the early days. Everything would be easy if we remained as we were—even justice would be easy—but we are no longer simple. You yourself have enriched our lives, and with our abundance we are no longer simple."

"I wanted abundance for everyone; that is why I taught new skills. I always wanted the riches to be distributed according to need. I appointed you for that job."

"Do not be afraid, Quetzalcoatl, if the needs are different. When we were few, it was easy to find in simplicity that which made us equal, and which we now find difficult because we are different. We are many, and it is impossible to succeed in the manner you desire. I believe that what is important in these moments is for someone to give orders and for others to obey, if great things are to be achieved in this world."

"No, Topiltzin, no. It is not enough to give orders; it has to be done with justice; each one should be given what is his."

"Very well," Topiltzin replied. "What belongs to the Toltecs, what they need to be sacred, to justify their passage through this land, is the pyramid that will be built as you conceived it to sustain our greatness and that of the twin."

"I have paid a dear price," Quetzalcoatl thought. "I consented to the violent conquest of the Chichimecs; but now that I have become aware of it, I cannot consent to the suffering of so many people. I will gather them together and listen to them. In things that pertain to many the opinions of one are not enough; it is necessary to listen to many in order to alleviate the suffering of all."

"We do not need to hear them, Quetzalcoatl. We Toltecs are the owners of the land; we are the ones who know and command. Why give that up?"

"These are things which concern us all. Are we not all men made and organized in the same way?"

"They may all be men; but they are not Toltecs. You have chosen to live with this people, we received you here, we became great with you, and we are now the best and will continue to be so, according to our destiny. We govern and there is no reason why we should give up our government. No one guarantees us that a different justice will be superior to ours. If you are speaking of justice, it is justice that I demand for the Toltecs, as we already command and know. Those are the facts. We should not have to receive the same treatment as others."

"It is necessary," Quetzalcoatl replied, "in order to find the good that can protect us all."

"Think carefully, Quetzalcoatl, lest you should cause the first displeasure to the people who love you, who followed you, who have grown with you and have received you in their hearts. They love you and you love them, you have taught them, and they still follow you in everything."

"Your words, so full of arrogance, create a great disturbance in my spirit, Topiltzin. They frighten me because I fear them to be the voice of a rich people. I have never felt your displeasure before. I never thought that words and deeds could come out of us and wander in the world as your sons, alone and far from us, until they arrived at places we had not imagined. How far is all this from my intentions! It is truly difficult to build a pyramid. But listen to me, Topiltzin! This pyramid that is being built for the twin will not have infamy as its foundation. I will impose justice by means of a new order!"

"This is not justice for the Toltecs, and we will allow nothing against Tula, not even from Quetzalcoatl," Topiltzin concluded.

Quetzalcoatl was shocked, and Topiltzin left with the important men, who were patting him on the back.

Quetzalcoatl remained alone, sad and worried. Tatle found him in this condition and asked:

"What worries you, Father Quetzalcoatl? What star is moving in the skies in a way that does not meet your calculations?"

"It is not the stars that worry me, Tatle, it is men. The stars, in their rigid beauty, had made me forget men. After all, they follow a fixed course whose law they obey and which we must learn in order to know how they will continue to move; but men do not respond to fixed laws. I can calculate nothing with my threads and my figures.

"The star we live on follows a regular course; but the men who live on it form their behavior in an arbitrary way. Now they want one thing and tomorrow they will want another. Today they despise what they sought yesterday. Some love, others hate; some give, others take; and tomorrow it will all be different. Despite its regularity, this world is a confused sphere of arbitrary things."

"You are right," Tatle agreed. "I do not understand the

world of men, even though I am one of them. Often I do not even understand what happens inside myself. I hate them all, but I also love them. There are days when I cannot bear to be spoken to, and I would give my life for any of them. I try to be their equal in some way, and yet an element of difference appears in everything."

"Do not worry, Tatle, it is the youth in you that deprives you of your serenity. We are equal because we are all brothers. We were all born and we shall all die through the same Creator. We all struggle to survive and to be better. And tell me, Tatle, can you say that one person has more right to live than another? What has happened to me now is that, as a result of studying the sky and teaching the things of the land, I have forgotten the Tree that I planted in the square. I have not cultivated it and it has borne no fruit for the Toltecs. Abundance has made them arrogant; wisdom, proud; richness, hard and merciless. And I have consented to it! Oh, Tatle! I have dreamt of leading and I do not know how to guide; I stumble everywhere and fall into every temptation. Only you, in the confusion of your youth and with your closeness to my life, try to understand me, despite your lack of serenity."

"You cannot say that, Quetzalcoatl. You have taken these people a long way. I have seen them grow and become powerful, always learning from your words, your intentions, and your deeds, as I, too, grew up and was no longer a child."

"It is easy for me to teach with my hands things relative to the land and its richness. My mind can understand the movement of the stars in the sky. But the human spirit in its depth and its complexity is beyond my understanding and I am confused. I have assumed that it is enough to speak and preach, disregarding the fact that words are soon forgotten. Not even with my own example have I been able to break that natural inclination which leads the strong to take advantage of their force and to act triumphant."

"I feel, Father Quetzalcoatl, that you are right, and yet I have often discussed this with Topiltzin without being able to counter his arguments. They ask me, and I ask myself: Why shouldn't the strong enjoy the greatness of the land? They know how to obtain its treasures. Why share them with the helpless, the old, the imbeciles, and the sick? Do not all things in nature happen as they should? The unfortunate ones would contaminate the world of those who can speedily move ahead. Topiltzin has acquired great power, thanks to his own merit. He has great influence among the Toltecs and they obey him, and he only consults with you on the fundamental things, whose which he himself doubts. Why has the Creator constructed both the strong and the weak?"

"There is sense in what you say, Tatle. It is a serious question that can only be solved by the scale of merit, which is not a convincing argument but a feeling that strengthens one's heart. Tell me, who has more merit: the powerful who strips the weak by taking advantage of his strength, or the one who restores and keeps nothing, even though he could do so because he took it in the first place? The weak, the sick, the incapable are despised. Who passes judgment? If the powerful does so because of his strength, later on he will be judged by a greater power. We are all men, and one identical light, the light of our life and our endurance, moves along illuminating the corners of the infinite, while we are nestled in our own time. That is the light that matters, and it is lit for all the living. What is force compared to conscience? Nothing more than the weight of a stone! Each conscience watches over and illuminates the work of

67

God from a point that no one can replace. Do not doubt. Maintain your conviction to serve! And remember that there is more merit in using your force for the benefit of the suffering than for your own gain!"

"It may be as you say, Quetzalcoatl. I have not been able to articulate it. Merit! Merit! A strange word that only makes sense in the world of men. You have frequently spoken to me about it. Where will the merit with which we burn our lives go? Will it also rise, like copal, like pain, to strengthen the gods? Will it be the offering that nourishes the creator's immobility?"

"Yes, Tatle, it will! It is the scale on which the best of the universe is weighed. It is the scale based on guilt and innocence, love and pain, light and darkness, which sustains merit. On it we ourselves are weighed."

"It is a scale that wounds my flesh and my soul, Quetzalcoatl, because I cannot weigh myself!'

"You will learn, Tatle! And then you will have the satisfaction that will cause you the most pain! Look at me now, oppressed by the weight of the pyramid. My love for Ce-Acatl and the vanity of my own importance led me to allow the Toltecs to build it in order to raise them from the sadness of my defeat and the sorrow and surprise at Acatl's death! It is a horrible monument to my arrogance, built with the pain and the blood of the miserable and the defeated! But I will find a remedy for it!"

The pyramid was in an advanced stage of construction when Quetzalcoatl called Topiltzin and the important men. They did not attend. He called them for three days and still they did not come. On the fourth, he went to look for them and found them in the palaces that Topiltzin had built with the labor of his Chichimec servants.

"To what an extent have I removed my eyes from the earth to study the course of the stars!" Quetzalcoatl thought. He said: "Your dwelling is beautiful, Topiltzin!"

"It was from you that I learned how to build it, Quetzalcoatl!"

"I built the house of the heart of the people and I was taken there so that I would live."

"I have put up my own home for the rest and rejoicing of my heart. I have fought too much and I have too many wounds not to have a place to rest in."

'Heroes need rest, Topiltzin! You must have been tired when you did not answer my call!"

"I have wanted time to pass, Quetzalcoatl, so that you would reflect and have no reason to be annoyed. I have spoken with my companions about the greatness of Tula and about your own plans, and we have decided that the greatness of Tula will prevail over your beautiful words. No one but the Toltecs will rule this land. Only their laws will be obeyed! We have arrived and this is where we shall stay. We want to remain on the top like the snow on the tall mountains of Anahuac."

"I have said nothing and already there is arrogance in your words and unnecessary energy in your gestures. We have known each other and walked together for too long to have our harmony destroyed now."

"We do not destroy it, Quetzalcoatl! We are still the same, the Toltecs, the people you chose to build the greatness of Anahuac, and who will not give up what they already have!"

69

"But I have given it to them! And it is fair that I should want it for the rest!"

"You see, Quetzalcoatl, you are the one who has changed! I acknowledge—and it would be wrong not to—that you have taught us everything we know. Do not deprive your achievement of merit by demanding a payment that was not stipulated. We were the ones who learned, and worked, and suffered. And now you ask us to give what is ours to strengthen savages whom we have already defeated, to put our own throats under the knives that we ourselves will hand over. You want us to distribute Tula's riches among all the people of Anahuac and to start again from dust! No! Let them start! And you can start with them, if that is what you want! Give them what is yours, do not deprive us of our own!"

"Be quiet, Topiltzin! Do not be insolent! I have not been able to speak. You don't want to listen and you look at me as though you'd like to hit me in the mouth! I only demand justice for everyone. It grieves me that Tula's greatness should rest on the suffering of others. It grieves me that your arrogance should make you forget the human race, and that you should defend the idea of people remaining in need where there is overabundance!"

"You wanted it as much as we, Quetzalcoatl! Do not let your compassion poison your intentions and forget your chosen people."

"I have no chosen people, Topiltzin! I love the ones who came first as much as those who came last! I want to give them all the same reward!"

"Quetzalcoatl betrays us! Quetzalcoatl loves the Chichimecs who broke his jaw! Quetzalcoatl loves our enemies! Quetzalcoatl denies his people! Quetzalcoatl has lost his mind by watching so many stars and having no women!"

"Be silent, Topiltzin!" and he slapped him in the mouth with the back of his hand.

There was a tense and vibrating silence.

Quetzalcoatl left in a rage. No one followed him. They all gathered around Topiltzin and, comforting him, said: "Quetzalcoatl has changed! He no longer is the Quetzalcoatl of the Toltecs! He is the arrow of the Chichimecs!"

Through his followers, Quetzalcoatl gathered the various peoples at the foot of the great pyramid, which was rising towards the sky. He warned them that he would probably be hindered and that, one way or another, as many people as possible should gather at the appointed time, that very day before sunset.

There he was, enraged, surrounded by his loyal followers. Tatle, bewildered and trembling with emotion, stood on his right. Gradually the people arrived; some, pursued by their masters who became still at the sight of Quetzalcoatl; others surreptitiously; and still others, accompanied by Toltecs who did not know what had happened.

When a great number had gathered, Quetzalcoatl raised his hands and said: "People of Anahuac! Quetzacoatl wants to speak to all of you and communicate to you his affliction, his sorrow, and his grief!

"I find suffering where I wished to bring happiness!

"I find misery where I have brought abundance!

"There is an abyss of hatred and enmity where I wished to build harmony.

"Now I realize, and I cry out my complaint!

"I want to tell everyone that I belong to all and that the

riches we have gathered, symbolized by this pyramid, belong to all Anahuac!

"I curse the whip and the stroke!

"I curse injustice!

"I curse misery!

"And now I announce a new order that I will impose in this land, which will shelter everyone and for which I will need everyone's agreement and good will. I speak especially to the Toltecs who are now listening to me in bewilderment. Fear nothing if you are just; I shall make you richer if you learn how to give. The new order will greatly need the Toltecs, who love me, for without them it will be hard to build anything in these lands. Let us make one people of all who are different, and we shall all be brothers seeking the same purpose.

"Quetzalcoatl will lead the whole Anahuac, with no distinctions, to a world of abundance and justice.

"Go and say this to the ones who have not come, and announce that tomorrow, at sunrise in this same place, we shall gather to make a new agreement."

After he had spoken, a Chichimec named Maxtla timidly asked:

"Powerful Quetzalcoatl, lord of the Toltecs, may I say something in the name of my people?"

"Speak!" said Quetzalcoatl.

"Give us freedom, not abundance! We were far away in our own lands, we were our own masters, and now we are subjected to this cruel servitude. We have spent years dragging stones and piling earth to erect a mound for a god that is alien to us! Our life is hard because we have learned to realize how low we are and how, like the dust, we are trod upon. You govern in Tula, you command your army! You ordered our captivity! Everything is done on your orders! Give orders for our liberty! We want to return to our own land and to run after deer and buffalo more than we want any justice or any good that you may give us."

"There is truth in what you say," Quetzalcoatl interrupted. "It is my repentance that speaks, and because of it I want to make amends for the harm I have done. I want to give abundance, riches, and a good life to make up for past sorrows!"

"We are not interested in your life or in your riches. We do not want the servitude in which the Toltecs live in order to provide themselves with what you call a good life."

"I shall give you happiness!" Quetzalcoatl cried.

"Then give us freedom! Who can judge happiness? Who can decide what happiness we want? Why should it be you who teaches how to carve the stones that are carried on our bloody backs? It is not the bland life of the Toltecs that we want! We want no *teponaxtles,* no flutes, nor the stinking smell of the great crowds packed into villages! We want to be the masters of our own happiness! We want to feel the happiness of the arrow shot into the air, free as the wind! That is what we want, Quetzalcoatl—not this life full of artifice with which the Toltecs cover their nakedness! Give us freedom!"

"How is it possible that the Chichimecs think this way?" Quetzalcoatl said. "I will give you security, well-being, rest; I will ornament your life with the things that make it pleasing. Out there, the Chichimec dies young in his maddening chase after the animals he eats, eats if he manages to catch them and not perish in the attempt. Here we live from the land, with the regularity of the seasons, waiting for its fruits."

"Let us die our own death! Our life may be brief and crude, but it is ours! Our death may be premature, but it is ours! Give us freedom, scourge of the Chichimecs! Give us freedom, and may we never again hear of you, of your justice, of your repentance, or of these builders of pyramids!"

Quetzalcoatl was about to answer when suddenly he was surrounded by a group of warriors, while others attacked the crowd, beating and pushing them.

"To work! No more speeches or rebukes! There is too much to be done for this conversation between the Quetzalcoatl of the Chichimecs and Maxtla, the rebel, to continue!"

"Get back, Toltec warriors!" Quetzalcoatl cried. "Do not stain your hands with the blood of defenseless prisoners! Get back! Get back!" His followers tried to break the barrier and failed. They were soon taken. Only Tatle escaped, and he ran to where Maxtla was screaming in a terrible way that stirred the hearts of the Chichimecs. His screams were like the sounds of the coyote and the jaguar, and they awoke the ancient instinct for savage battle among his companions.

"Let us go to our land, Chichimecs! Let us go! Fight! Kill! Die! But let us go!" and he thrust himself against the guards, hitting them with whatever he could find. His companions did likewise and his cries encouraged those who had not yet come.

The battle spread. Many Chichimecs were captured and others killed. But nothing could halt the stampede of those who ran out of the city, crying out as they sensed freedom. Among them went Tatle, holding Maxtla who was wounded.

The Toltec warriors, though armed, were unable to keep up the pursuit and soon sunset, and later night, swallowed up the tireless fugitives. Their cries echoed more and more distantly in the night.

Peace returned to Tula. The guards were reinforced and Quetzalcoatl, deprived of his followers, was tied to a post and led in captivity to a room in the house of the heart of the people, where he remained a prisoner.

A year after these events, thirteen years after the beginning of its construction, the pyramid was completed according to Quetzalcoatl's plan. Four stone giants that resembled Ce-Acatl supported the roof at the top.

In that year, the Toltecs became used to the new state of affairs and they consecrated the pyramid to the precious twin with great feasts. Many quetzal birds were sacrificed to the serpent so that Quetzalcoatl would regain his reason and would love his people again. The feathers were taken to the prison as ornaments. And it was in this way that the great pyramid of the Toltecs was built. At that time one twin was in the skies, and the other a prisoner.

CHAPTER VI

❦

The Captives

HE WAS TAKEN to the house of the heart of the people. He arrived sad and emaciated. He had broken the post and had freed himself from the ropes that bound him.

"Let nothing bind me except time and the will of the Toltecs. Time for rebellion and time for choosing a way." He did not want to be carried.

"I shall walk, *Cocomes,*" he told his group. "It is time to walk barefooted again, feeling the dust between my toes. I am going into captivity and I wish to do so barefooted to understand the dimensions of this earth. I came to this house badly wounded. Now I come to it as a prisoner," and he took off his tunic and threw it away from him. The warriors who had custody of him, loyal to Topiltzin, looked at no one. They seemed to be somber mannequins. The oldest woman among the *Cocomes* picked up the tunic and rushed to the house, which was already surrounded by warriors.

"Quetzalcoatl has been made a prisoner!" she shouted to the other women, who started to cry at the sight of him, in the distance, surrounded by the guards, barefooted, arms dangling at his sides, his beard in tangles.

"Our lord is coming as a captive!"

"Let us cry!" said the old woman. "He wanted to be a judge and he has been condemned! Our pillar is coming as a captive! I do not understand the things that have happened: the people against the people; the people against their lord; the lord against everyone. I am afraid, sons! I am afraid! Let us cry for the Toltecs! Let us cry for Quetzalcoatl! Here we are imprisoned by the ones we love. Let us cry for everyone; for what is not understood; for the flood that comes upon us when everything was quiet and tame! Let us cry, daughters, for the cries of Quetzalcoatl that his people have not heard. Let us cry for the sorrow of the Toltecs! Bewilderment and fear. Bewilderment and fear are what the Toltecs suffer. Their father, their way, and their truth are in furious confusion. Let us cry for the sorrow of the son who struggles against his father. Let us cry for those who are right and for those who are mistaken. Let us cry, *Cocomes,* our lord is a captive of his own people!" And they all cried in anguish and bewilderment.

He entered the house while they lamented, and was locked up in one of the rooms, separated from his followers. He remained isolated. Only the old woman and a young one were allowed to take care of him and to feed him. It was in this way that, in solitude and captivity, Quetzalcoatl discovered the world of woman.

For several days he did not speak and hardly ate. The two women followed him with their eyes as he walked endlessly to and fro. They imagined his suffering.

"Eat! Eat, my lord," they would say to him. "Nourishment is necessary to keep the body alive. Eat, if only to strengthen your suffering heart! Feed your pain," they begged him. And they brought food close to his mouth and, begging in this way, they remained still for a long while looking at his face. He was alone most of the time.

"I am as alone as when I was born, as when I arrived on the bank. Alone as I will be when I must leave. It is an opportunity to look for myself. Acatl, my brother, has already gone. Tatle, my son, has already left me." And looking for himself, he was unable to find God. There was only a horrible silence, a boundless silence that filled him with terror.

"What a terrible judge is the silence of solitude when one is discontent with one's self!"

And he would remain still for hours, sullen, not looking for a consolation for his pain, not even choosing penance. A tight knot tied his silence to his inactivity. He was at torture's limit without crossing it, and he would remain like this until the soft presence of the two women surrounded him with their soft movements, voices, and hands. Some days went by. One morning, unexpectedly, a large group of important men burst into the room and broke the silence of his captivity. Topiltzin was not among them.

Quetzalcoatl was seated. He neither rose nor saw them. His eyes were lost in the distance. Huemac went up to him after a long silence.

"Quetzalcoatl," he said. For a long time the name vibrated in the room. He could say nothing else. There was anguish, sadness, and anxiety in all.

He stood up slowly and spoke softly, as though talking to the two women:

"What is it? Are you here to sentence me? Have you come to kill me? Do the Toltecs come as Quetzalcoatl's judges? Do they come as executioners in the middle of the morning? Evidently the time for passing judgment has come. Here I am, Toltecs. Alone before you! Alone before my shattered mission. Broken like a flint cracked by a stone. My freedom is broken. My will is dead, with dangling hands, absorbed in the dread of my silence. What do the Toltecs want from this broken flint? They want punishment, they want to turn him into dust! Of course! Punishment! They want to announce to Anahuac that the majesty of Tula retained its balance by Quetzalcoatl's punishment. Oh! The serenity of justice! The peace of justice! Brother punishes brother! Oh! The punishment, the sorrow with which the judge makes the people drunk! What do the Toltecs want of Quetzalcoatl? Do they want him to die? Do they want him to suffer? Quetzalcoatl is so sad that he will not be able to die or to suffer."

There was another long silence filled with anguish. "No, Quetzalcoatl!" Huemac replied. "We cannot be your judges. We have no law for you, nor do we have any punishment! What has happened is that you have fallen on top of us and destroyed us! Tula is silent without your presence! The silence fills us with awe! We are divided and full of dread! In the depths of our broken hearts we do not know what is to be done with Quetzalcoatl and we have come for you to decide. There is no other judge in this cause.

"Quetzalcoatl, what should the Toltecs do with you? What must Tula do with Quetzalcoatl? We want to know your answer, to learn what Quetzalcoatl will do with Tula! Why have you abandoned us, Quetzalcoatl? Why did you fall on your people like a god? Why have you broken what cannot be put together again? What happened? Why? Why?"

"You ask me, Huemac! I hardly know! It is like a brightness that I have inside. There are days in which my heart is on fire out of love for my brothers, for all men, and I would like to give to them all. Then I feel the terrible strength of my destiny, the power of the one who sows seed, and my will bursts and it goes out everywhere! It goes and comes like a wave on the beach, and it consumes me, wounds me, and nearly kills me! But there are also days when my heart freezes in the cold immensity of Teuhtlampa, and I am compressed within myself. I feel my insignificance and the smallness of my actions, and the thousands of eyes in the sky are the only ones that vibrate and seem important. I leave the earth and abandon its sorrows that seem to me like grains of sand that have little value in the enormity of the universe. And it is so until I see a tear, as brilliant as a star, and then my soul is kindled again and I overflow along all the roads. I am a guide who leaves and gets lost, who returns and stumbles. I am the lash of the Anahuac. That is why, Toltecs! That is why!"

"Then," they asked, "what shall we do with Quetzalcoatl!"

"Yes," Huemac said, "you weigh so heavily on us!" And he added: "But you also impede us! We are crushed! Tula does not know what to do!"

"I do know what to do with this body full of anguish and storms! I do know what to do with myself! Curse Quetzalcoatl! Curse the hour in which he came to Anahuac with his world of sin and repentance, with his hands full of temptations and his heart full of love! Curse this twin, the one who did not jump into the fire! I do know what to do with myself! Yet I tell you I do not want to die despite it all. I shall stay here, in my solitude, until I find the right time for my death. I shall lock myself up here, Toltecs! But I say one thing: I want to live. I want to go on seeing my hands, even if they are clenched into fists. I want to go on living, even in my solitude. I want to continue being someone. I want to feel that I am still on the earth, to rest my naked feet upon it and to have my eyes fixed on the stars! I want to continue being in the middle of all things. That is what I want! But I will not disturb the people I love anymore! I shall remain here. I shall not leave this place. The Toltecs will at last be left to their own decisions. That is my judgment, Huemac. That is my decision. Now go and tell Topiltzin that nothing is to be feared from Quetzalcoatl; that I shall stay here, alone and apart. Some day the Toltecs will find another cause and then perhaps Quetzalcoatl will be able to give them what they ask for, and not what his own arrogance suggests!"

"May it so be," said the important men. "Tula accepts the sentence! Quetzalcoatl will remain captive and alone until he finds the right time for his death!"

They informed Topiltzin and, although he accepted the sentence, he felt anxious because he felt that many of his companions already wanted to govern.

Quetzalcoatl remained alone until the two women went to see him at night. "Why is my lord Quetzalcoatl happy?" asked Cihuatl, the young one. She had never seen a smile in his eyes since he had been imprisoned.

"I smile because I have been my own judge and set my own sentence! Because I have found a way that leads nowhere!"

Cihuatl's heart was filled with happiness and she also laughed, and the old woman laughed too.

"Laugh and sing," said Quetzalcoatl. "Sing songs of this

land that I love so much. Sing because Quetzalcoatl has already been tried!"

"And what was the sentence?" the old woman asked anxiously, while Cihuatl stopped the song she had begun.

"I shall remain here as a captive. Only you, or others like you, will come to bring me sustenance and care."

"It will be us!" Cihuatl said in an anxious and decided way.

"And how long will my lord remain captive?" the old woman asked.

"Until I find the right time for my death!"

"Death! Death! Always death!" the old woman said in a low voice. "Always hovering around us like a starving coyote! Always looking at us with its empty eyes, its hairless head, and its laugh!"

"But my lord cannot die!" said Cihuatl. "He is different! I cannot imagine that he can die, I do not think he has a skull! My lord is very beautiful! He will not die! The sentence will not be carried out!"

"No, Cihuatl, everything perishes. Quetzalcoatl will also arrive at his place; he cannot and must not be immortal!"

"But my lord is a god who has come from far away!"

"No, Cihuatl! I am not a god! I am a mortal man. Look closely at my hand; it is the hand of a man who came on a stormy night, who has fallen many times, and who will depart at the end of his time." And Cihuatl softly held Quetzalcoatl's hand for a long time, with tears in her eyes. She placed it on her forehead and did not let go.

"My lord is a god and he will not die!"

"To die! To die! It is a strange thing to think of when everything in my being throbs, even the strange satisfaction of being tried."

"And what is death?" Cihuatl asked.

83

"I have felt it as a grey buzzing," Quetzalcoatl replied.

"And then," Cihuatl continued, "shall we be what we are?"

"I do not know, Cihuatl! I do not know! That is the doubt that has always stopped me from dying. Shall I be the one I am? Shall you be the one you are now? Tell me, Cihuatl, what do you think?"

"I have been taught that if I die giving birth, I shall go to a beautiful place full of delicious pleasures, in the company of my sons."

"If you die. But if you live? What of conduct? Will death be the one to give resurrection? Will it be life? This is a strange world in which, as I see it, death and not life shapes our future destiny! Here, if a soldier dies in battle, if he dies covered with wounds, he goes to a place full of delicious pleasures, no matter how he has lived. And life, Cihuatl! And life full of memory, full of moments, lived between good and bad. Does it not matter? Does only death matter?"

"I think it is very important to die," Cihuatl said, "even more than being born, when our mother helps and protects us. She suffers, and we only feel cold; but we feel no lack of protection. In death, my lord, we are alone."

"Alone, yes, alone. Alone in the middle of all things and, at the same time, at the end of what we are. I doubt, and that is why I do not die."

"Death is only an old and hungry coyote that turns into many things," the old woman added, "an old and mangy coyote that I would like to kill!"

"Kill death! It would be curious! And what for?" Quetzalcoatl asked.

"So I won't die!" the old woman said. "I am like you, I do not want to die!"

"There will be a day when you will not want to live.

There will be a day when I will not want to live. Until then, let us allow your coyote to live."

"I shall always want to live," the old woman concluded.

"And you, Cihuatl?" Quetzalcoatl asked.

"I shall want to live while my lord lives! If, as you say, you should die, I would also die. But Quetzalcoatl will not die, will he?"

"Yes, Cihuatl, Quetzalcoatl will die."

"Then I would like to make you immortal," Cihuatl told him.

And the three were silent.

After thinking for a long while, the old woman said:

"And why do you not make him immortal?"

"I? How?"

"Give him sons!" she said, and she rose and left them alone.

It was in this way that on the night of the day of his sentence, Quetzalcoatl fell into the temptation of becoming immortal, and he understood the intimate truth of Omeyocan, the Second Place, where everything is two, so as to be one and to know itself as two. It was then he discovered that within him were beating entire universes that changed places in the darkness of his entrails and turned into a tempest of brightness and lightning, precisely in the middle of the universe where one dies and lives, precisely in the center of all mists.

By Cihuatl he had two children, a boy and a girl. When the latter was born, the mother died.

Tatle was the other captive. He ran with the Chichimecs deep into the night. The cries had ceased and the only things that could be heard were the sound of heels and panting. Their collective escape had lasted until sunrise when they all stopped, for Maxtla had fallen several times and was dying.

"Maxtla is dying!" cried Tatle, gasping. "Let us stop to help him."

Bewildered by their freedom, in the silence of the fog-filled plain, with their feet wet with dew, they realized they could not stop. And they saw the ashen and agonized face of Maxtla, who had lost a great deal of blood. Stopping, he felt the throbbing of his heart in his temples as the sun, rising over the entire plain, resembled a flight across the horizon.

"He is about to die," many said. "He needs no help, he is dying alone. Let us go! Let us go!" and they hastened on their way.

"We cannot leave him here like an animal!" Tatle protested. "He was the one who asked, he was the one who encouraged the escape. We must help him!"

"We cannot stop! We are being followed! We have to reach the hills today!" many said.

"Let us build a stretcher and carry him," Tatle suggested.

"We would not be able to run. They would catch up with us. He will die. He already is ashen. Let us go! Let us go! Let us go!" they urged.

"But he was the one who guided you, who led you! You cannot leave him in the midst of the plain to be eaten by the buzzards!"

"He was only the voice of the Chichimecs. We all think the same, anyone could have said it. We all wanted to go. The Chichimecs have no leader. We are all free. He is free. It is not a custom of the Chichimecs to carry the dying. He is free and he will die. Let us go! Let us go!"

And they all left except Tatle, trembling with cold and

fatigue, and Maxtla's son, who was Tatle's age and stayed to be with his father at his death.

The Chichimecs continued their silent flight, tirelessly running while their shadows were lost in the morning haze.

A silence as thick as fog covered the three who stayed behind in the dew-covered weeds. The only sound was Maxtla's difficult breathing.

Neither Tatle nor the young man could do anything but wait for death's arrival. They laid him on the ground so he would be comfortable and placed weeds under his head. They washed his wounds with the wet weeds and waited for the sun to warm him.

"What can we do, Tatle?"

"Nothing, brother, nothing. We should not leave him alone. He must know that we are with him at the time of his death, that we shall gather his last breath, and that we shall go on living afterwards. Until then, this is where we shall stay, chasing away the buzzards so that they will not pluck out his eyes before his time. That is all we can do!"

The flight of the Chichimecs could still be seen in the distance. They remained squatting, watching him die.

In the morning the sun's warmth awoke the man, who asked for water. They were not able to give it to him. There was no water on the plain, and even if there had been, there was nothing in which to carry it. He asked for water until his mouth was swollen. Squatting, they watched and heard him dying. Once in a while they would scare away the flies that buzzed in the silence of the plain. The buzzards circled above but had not descended. They did not know if Maxtla was aware that they were accompanying him at his time of death. Night came to the plain and with it, cold. They huddled by the wounded man to keep him warm. He died at dawn while they were sleeping. They did not know the time of his death. With the light of the new day, they realized he was already rigid and drenched with dew, like the weeds. They ran in search of water for themselves before the buzzards began their descent.

While he ran, still imagining the dead man drenched with dew, Tatle realized he was running away from Quetzalcoatl, and he began to cry because he loved him dearly. He ran in front of the other young man and tears wet his cheeks. No one, except himself, knew that he was crying, as no one finds the source of the water that drips from the high peaks in the mountains. By escaping from Quetzalcoatl, which was nearly like escaping from himself, from the sorrow of his youth torn by the two halves, he ran to the world of elementary freedom. In it he remained captive, a prisoner of his own self, of his own solitude.

He learned the agonizing torture of hunger and thirst; the painful running after prey and away from danger. Loneliness and fear. Loneliness and fear that leave no time for thinking, only fatigue, pain, or cold. Only once, after an exhausting chase after a fawn which they finally caught and ate, did he speak with the young man about things that did not pertain to their daily sustenance. They were satiated and rested.

"Why did you come with us?" the young man asked. "You did not need to escape!"

"I wanted the life of the Chichimecs. Your father spoke so passionately about freedom, and you all looked so weak that I wanted to come with you. But I did not find the Chichimecs."

"There are no Chichimecs," the young man said. "We are not 'the', we are each 'one.' We gather and we disperse. We help each other and we separate. We are like the air that disperses, like the arrow that goes on its way alone, even if it was once with others in the quiver. We have no leaders or guides, no priests. I think you were thinking of leading the Chichimecs as your lord has led the Toltecs."

"Perhaps that is right, perhaps that is what I wanted to do. I saw you weak and persecuted. Perhaps I wanted to guide you. Now I realize that true freedom is its own guide. The Chichimecs left, and now the ones who are not dead are free."

"That is true," said the young man. "Now you are also free because you are not a leader."

"Yes," Tatle concluded. "Now I am free!"

On the following day he fell down an embankment and broke his leg. The young man found him at the bottom and waited for him to regain consciousness.

"Your leg is shattered," he said. "You will not be able to run, you will not be able to hunt!"

"Help me!" Tatle begged.

"I do not know how. I have already tried to help my father and I could not even know the time of his death. I shall be on my way!" And he left, leaving Tatle alone.

"Now I am truly free!" he said. "But I will not die! Especially alone. I do not want to die!" And he made a great effort to live.

He looked for other men, but he did not want to return to Tula with a crippled leg. And dragging himself from valley to valley, eating herbs and roots, suffering great hardships, he finally came to the caves inhabited by the priests who had abandoned Tula and were waiting to return. And among them, once again, he lost his freedom and became a captive of the company of men. On his way he had discovered the hallucinations induced by peyote and other herbs he had eaten in the desperation of hunger and thirst. His mind became open to the multicolored and unreal world that was liberated by the overflowing effect of this vegetable stimulation. Within him were created universes full of feathers and serpents, and he taught their use to the ones who received him and he was respected because of this. They called him the Cripple of the Hallucinations.

CHAPTER VII

❦

The Drought

A YEAR AFTER the beginning of Quetzalcoatl's captivity, a great drought began which continued for seven years and dried up the land of Anahuac.

It was then that Quetzalcoatl was beginning his captivity and his own time of sowing.

Full of pride, it was the old woman who made it public:

"Our lord Quetzalcoatl, who is captive, has sown his seed in the womb of one of our virgins! At last Anahuac will know the sons of Quetzalcoatl's blood, at last Quetzalcoatl will be immortalized in our race." And all the *Cocomes* entered excitedly and made great feasts in the intimacy of the house of the heart of the people.

Cihuatl was taken to a separate place and treated with great care. As she left the house and walked across the village, the pregnant women touched her belly and showered her with blessings.

Topiltzin was concerned. "Quetzalcoatl has taken a woman," he said. "Now he will become rooted in the land. He has taken strength from one of our virgins. Quetzalcoatl does not want to die. Now more than ever he will want to live: we will have more problems and we will not know what to do with his cubs. They will be like jaguars and they will want to devour the Toltecs. Let us kill them in time!"

"It is your resentment that makes you think that way," Huemac replied to him. "On the contrary, Quetzalcoatl now gives the Toltecs his blood along the roads of love, not through hate. Now we will be his brothers, through his work, through his real children who will be given birth by one of our women, through her own pain. Now Quetzalcoatl will really be ours, he will truly belong to this land where his harvest will be reaped. We shall win Quetzalcoatl again. We shall not kill his children, because they are ours too, as he himself will again be."

"We do not need him any longer," said Topiltzin. "We already know everything and have gone further than he has, as he is always trapped in the fog of his compassion, always thinking of others and not about us, as we want him to."

"There must be a reason. He must want to teach us something through his fatherhood," Huemac said.

"The dry tree of Quetzalcoatl can no longer teach us anything," Topiltzin replied.

"Now it will have new shoots for us. Ce-Acatl will be happy; new feathers will be born for Anahuac. They will be Quetzalcoatl's children, new links with the Toltecs. He broke the old ones; now he is repairing them. We owe a great deal to Quetzalcoatl and Tula should expect even more."

"We should have killed him before he had children," murmured Topiltzin. "They will be neither one thing nor the other. They will be more confused than poor Tatle's soul, always so full of words, always looking for things he cannot find. I think we should kill Quetzalcoatl's children."

"No," Huemac protested, "they are also Toltecs and we

no longer perform sacrifices. That was the first agreement with Quetzalcoatl."

"It would not be a sacrifice," said Topiltzin, "it would be a means of prevention."

"It would be a sacrifice to your fear and resentment; you are confused, Topiltzin. You used to love Quetzalcoatl. You followed him. You saved him from the Chichimecs. And suddenly, when you began to taste the power that we have given you, you began to hate him. Something happened within you that even you do not understand. You are like Tatle, you are disturbed inside!"

"I do not hate him, I no longer need him and I know very well what I want, and I am not like Tatle, that somber child. I am a man who wants to take Tula's power far, to the two seas. Tula has a great future in store. I want to make the Toltecs greater."

"Quetzalcoatl wanted that same thing!"

"It is not true!" said Topiltzin. "Quetzalcoatl does not love the Toltecs, Quetzalcoatl loves men and men do not exist! There are Toltecs, or there are Chichimecs; the builders or the savages; but there are no men. Nothing can be done for what does not exist. Mere words, mere concepts. Men! A lie in Quetzalcoatl's mouth, the shield for a compassion that has prevented Tula from advancing. You have already seen what happened with the Chichimecs that Quetzalcoatl tried to lead; they went after their freedom, destroying Tula's order!"

"I think," Huemac said, "that what Quetzalcoatl wanted was to make Toltecs out of the Chichimecs, in the same way that he wanted to make his sons Toltecs. Perhaps there will be a day when we will all be Toltecs and belong to the same race. I think that is what Quetzalcoatl wants."

"Now you too are playing with words! It is Quetzalcoatl's

influence, full of words and more words. He is going to have children of his blood! But how many children of his word has he had?"

"They may be words, Topiltzin, but you fear them. You are afraid of Quetzalcoatl. All his children frighten you. I think you even fear me! What are you afraid of, Topiltzin?"

"I fear nothing, Huemac, and you even less!"

"Then leave us all in peace, whether Quetzalcoatl's children in blood or in word! And leave yourself in peace, for you are the son of his deeds!"

"I am no one's son! I am the son of this land and I am not leaving anyone in peace! I think we should not let Quetzalcoatl's children be born."

But the important men opposed him, and Topiltzin agreed to have Cihuatl remain captive so that the people would not see Quetzalcoatl's children until it was known what they were like.

In this way it was possible for the first one to be born, a cub as fair as the sun. The older woman was the midwife and soon she was crying throughout the house:

"Our daughter has given birth to a son! There is a new son among us! He is the color of corn, even his hair is like the floss!"

The news spread beyond the house, and the people, who still loved Quetzalcoatl, were happy.

Topiltzin felt greatly disturbed and frightened.

Huemac felt happy.

Quetzalcoatl watched him being born like an ear of corn and he understood the mystery of the navel.

"Go and bury the cord in the middle of the land," he told the old woman. "May this innermost, mysterious bridge between generations, this funnel of the infinitely small in the infinitely large, link me closer to the land and to my lineage; may it project itself into time until we can all be one again." And turning to his son, who was crying on the lap of his panting mother, he said:

"Now that the cord has been broken we, who used to be two, are now three. Ineffable mystery of creation! Now, my son, you are someone! May God be thanked for your being. Blood, always blood! You have arrived between blood and pain, and your first breath is a gasp of tears. Now I understand that blood is both pain and love, the knot of a cord that rots in the middle of the earth. You were made, and you are already yourself; you are like me. You are made with the fibers of joy and sorrow, of laughter and tears. You are at the edge of all the possibilities, and soon you will have the strength to choose. You will be the course and the measure of richness and misery. You will be eagle and serpent. With your pain you will maintain the conscience of the universe, and with your laughter, the dignity of man. Because you will know how to laugh, my son, the very essence of liberation. And you will know how to dance and sing, to hold your own in the concert of Teuhtlampa. I know the hour of your birth; but I do not know where you come from, as I do not know what your destiny will be. You have arrived like me, like everyone before; like everyone along the obscure conduits of generation, until you burst into the light of your own conscience, which is the limit and the end of the infinite—one, only one—you alone, your irreducible self. Now you are someone, my son! And you cry. I shall cry with you!"

But the people did not know the child, did not see the mother. They only knew that Quetzalcoatl was a captive because he had provoked the rebellion of the Chichimecs, broken the order of Tula, and jeopardized its safety.

Exactly one year after the child's birth, the severity of the drought began to be felt.

That year the wind that precedes the rains hardly blew, and the rains were scarce, and the crops poor.

"The wind has not swept the road of rain," said the sowers of seed, and they began to grow sad.

"It is because Quetzalcoatl, in his feathered cloak, has not come to see how we prepare the land."

And there were some who began to say that the rain was also captive, like Quetzalcoatl's golden son.

But that year there were no major disasters. The granaries were still full and their abundance allowed Tula to continue living in opulence.

To divert the people's attention, Topiltzin began war campaigns against more and more distant lands, and products and prisoners were brought from afar.

At the same time, he ordered great houses to be built for the most aggressive leaders, and the leaders were content.

In the following year the rains were even more scarce, and it was not possible to water the crops with their reserves, for the canals had been abandoned and the water wasted. But Tula's abundance and the raids had not made the need apparent.

The idea became widespread that the imprisonment of the child who resembled an ear of corn was also holding the rain captive.

The following years were harder and the last ones were terrible, for as the reserves ran out, it became necessary to ration food. The surrounding villages, which also suffered, began looking toward Tula's riches to satisfy their needs. The Chichimecs were very close to Tula, whose armies, exhausted by constant fighting, were insufficient.

In the sixth year the situation became unbearable. Topiltzin's prestige had decayed, and he managed to remain in power by means of constant gifts to the leaders and the heads of the army. But the satisfaction of some and the needs of most, which became hunger and desperation, had Tula in a state of revolt.

Huemac led the discontented, and he organized the opposition that demanded the fair distribution of the reserves and the intervention of the captive Quetzalcoatl so that he would guide Tula along the roads of abundance again.

The crisis exploded in the seventh year. Harassed, powerless, with no troops, and order destroyed, Topiltzin had sent for the priests who had gone north, so that they could devise a remedy. The commission arrived on a silent night. They were plainly dressed in furs. Their straight hair was dirty, long, and foul-smelling. They arrived with arrogance.

"You called for us, Topiltzin, and here we are. We do not

know what the powerful Topiltzin, the devil's favorite son, wants us for. He has destroyed the tradition of the people, and he has built these houses to harbor the fondness of luxury that ails the sons of the land who, now called Toltecs, have forgotten the gods and have made their nonconformity evident. What do you want, Topiltzin?"

"I want it to rain! The people are in great need and have become anxious and rebellious. I am surrounded by enemies and traitors. Only by feeding the people will tranquillity and order return to Tula."

"Ask your Quetzalcoatl for water!"

"He is not mine! If he were, he would no longer be. . . . He is an absurd being who wanted to destroy Tula's power. That is why I have imprisoned him, together with his wife and children. But the people are restless and want to set him free. They say that the captivity of the firstborn, who resembles the color of tender corn, does not allow the ears to grow."

"Quetzalcoatl has children!" the bewildered priests said, and one of them added: "Then the gods' revenge could be great!"

"But tell us, Topiltzin, what is it that you want?"

"I want it to rain! The land is dry and cracked. Many people have died of hunger and thirst. What remains is booty for those who rob us. I want it to rain! I can do nothing as a soldier. I need magic, I need the gods. And that is why I sent for you."

"The drought also affects us," they answered. "And it is because Tezcatlipoca is enraged. All the land renders homage to the serpent, and no one performs sacrifices to Tezcatlipoca, except for us in the loneliness of our caves."

"What can I do? What must I do?" asked Topiltzin.

98

The wizards were silent for a long time and stared at Topiltzin, who began to feel uneasy.

"We need a great sacrifice!" they said.

"Let us do it!" Topiltzin answered.

"Give us Quetzalcoatl's firstborn!"

"So be it!" said Topiltzin joyfully.

"And prepare for our return!" the wizards concluded.

That same night Quetzalcoatl's firstborn was stolen and handed over to the wizards.

No one in Tula ever knew about the child whose hair was like the corn. Some said that he had been reborn in the land of the Itzas, far away, among the Maya, where they came to adore him as Ku-Kul-Kan.

And the old woman decided that she no longer wanted to live, and was happy that the Coyote had not died. She let herself die. She dried up.

When he realized the child had disappeared, Quetzalcoatl left his prison, and no one dared to stop him. So great was his sorrow that there were no words, and none were ever spoken. He looked for the child, and the child did not appear.

But it did not rain, and, what was worse, violent fires broke out in Tula.

When the people saw Quetzalcoatl again, they begged him, in tears, to do something so that the punishment that afflicted them would cease. But Quetzalcoatl did not hear— he only searched, and soon, so did the people who followed him.

Huemac joined the search and they all went to Topiltzin's palace.

"Give me my son!" said Quetzalcoatl in a broken voice. "Give him to me and I shall do what you want!"

"Die! Die!" Topiltzin screamed. And he hurled himself upon Quetzalcoatl. But Huemac intervened while the people entered the palace and hindered the movements of the guards.

"Leave me alone! Leave me alone!" Topiltzin roared.

"Return the child!" cried Huemac.

"I do not have that cursed cub, the master of the drought! I have given him to Tezcatlipoca so that abundance may return to Tula!" howled Topiltzin.

Quetzalcoatl became as violent as an eagle and with the strength of a serpent grasped Topiltzin's neck with his hands, and in front of everyone began to strangle him. When Topiltzin was about to die, he released him abruptly, passionately whispering: "It is not so! It is not so!" And he left, surrounded by the bewildered people.

"Water! Water!" the people pleaded.

"My son! My son!" Quetzalcoatl replied.

"Water! Water!" begged the people. "Our sons are thirsty and die of need! Our sons! Like your own!"

Then Quetzalcoatl heard the suffering of the people and saw the parents' tears, the same as his.

And, as many years ago, he ordered the people to gather, and with his great voice he said:

"Tula is thirsty! Little can I do for Tula, except uphold the faith. I lack the strength to find my son, but I shall uphold the faith. The ways of the winds and clouds are strange. I do not know if there is anything I can do. But I shall do what I must. It is not men's mission to bring rain. The order of the winds and the waters does not obey men. But I shall maintain the faith, go up to the pyramid, like Ce-Acatl, and there, at the highest point, I shall fast and bear the pain until it rains or until I die. I know no device to attract water, nor do I have access to the canals of the sky. I only know mortification when reason and craft reach the limit of their understanding and action. I can only offer the death I carry in my soul and the consumption of my body so that it may rain. Have faith, Toltecs, I uphold it. Either it rains, or I die! An absurd alternative, but it is the only one my grief and my helplessness can suggest, and I have faith." Saying no more, he slowly went up the pyramid and began the fasting that was to last for forty days.

Topiltzin no longer wanted power—not even the little he still had—amidst the hunger, the thirst, and the tears of the Toltecs. He felt the approach of death in his throat as a black buzzing, and lost interest in power.

"I no longer want to govern," he said. "The fruit of power is bitter when failure appears. Then everything is forgotten and the last step, the bad one, is the one that counts. I cannot command. There are powers that I no longer control. I do not know what to do! Only the one who can bring rain will govern here, and I cannot. That is the work of the gods and I have already done what I could."

"You have done a horrible thing!" answered Huemac. "You have broken the first agreement in the worst manner possible."

"The sacrifice had to be great," Topiltzin said.

"But it was not your sacrifice; you traded with another's grief. You only revealed your own resentment."

"You may be right," said Topiltzin. "But I do not repent! Someone in Tula had to suffer. In any case, I no longer want to govern!"

"No, Topiltzin! You no longer can govern! Little was the authority you had, and it was removed from you by your encounter with Quetzalcoatl. They all saw you defeated and pardoned."

"So they did! I think you should meet and decide what to do with me."

"We have met and we shall soon decide!"

After deliberating, they spoke to Topiltzin, who was squatting some distance away, with a forlorn look:

"We have decided, Topiltzin. You can no longer govern! You would not know how! We are handing you over to Quetzalcoatl so that he can deal with you as he pleases. We shall wait for things to happen, and in the meantime we shall all govern. So will it be."

"I do not care! Nothing matters to me any more!" said Topiltzin.

And they all went together to see Quetzalcoatl, who was

seated with crossed legs at the top of the pyramid, in front of the cross which he had planted, by a mud stove where copal burned. It was his fifth day of fasting and mortification.

Quetzalcoatl was becoming old. He had white hair, and wrinkles covered his temples. He had been in this land for twenty-six years and the people were still not used to his existence.

The leaders went up at sunset. They took Topiltzin with a rope tied around his neck. Quetzalcoatl was still, his eyes closed. A warm and soft evening breeze stirred his greying beard. It had been black before his captivity.

"Lord," said Huemac, "Topiltzin no longer governs the land. He no longer is the one who distributes or administers. He has no power and he does not want to have it—nor do we want him to. Now that you have returned among us, we bring him to you, tied up, for you to decide his fate."

"Release him. He is no wild beast. He is a confused man, defeated by power and life." And turning to Topiltzin he said to him softly: "Now I see you again as I did the first time, a long time ago, when you came for me in the hills, at the time of my first mortification. Then I was paying for my violence. Now I pay for the grief of this dry and blazing land. How much harm I have done you! How I must have disturbed your spirit for you to have found pleasure and necessity in destroying the existence of my first son! I have hardly thought of anything else. You are like this land to which I have brought trouble, while I felt like a fountain. I arrived before my time, like a lost spore that contaminates the sowing. I have done harm trying to do good. There may be someone who does good trying to do harm! What does it matter? What is important? Poor Topiltzin, thrown in front of his prisoner! Poor prisoner! Poor men of the earth, owners of a beautiful light in their conscience, and yet stumbling from grief to grief. This terrible world of creation. I do not understand! I do not understand the sorrow I did not seek! My son! The son of the Toltecs!"

Topiltzin said nothing. He was lying down, staring at the earth.

"What shall we do with Topiltzin?" the Toltecs insisted.

"Quetzalcoatl, the judge at his own trial?" he asked himself. "Shall I judge my own brother? Am I now the one who decides? And what is he charged with? With the loss of power? That already is a sentence!"

"Tell us what has to be done," they insisted.

"I can only be my own judge."

"But he killed your son!" they told him.

"My grief is too great for revenge," said Quetzalcoatl. "And justice does not comfort me. What is more: I want no consolation! I want to take all my grief and deliver it, with strong intention, so that water may return to this land. If intention counts in this world, if it has any merit, I want to suffer for this cause with all my intention so that water may return to Anahuac. Let there be no revenge or justice! Nothing to make my grief easier! Let it all be, so that water returns to the land! The sons of the Toltecs will satiate their thirst, or I will die. I am no judge, Toltecs! Leave me alone in my sacrifice so that I may not even have the satisfaction of speaking of it!"

Silent and respectful, they descended the pyramid. Topiltzin went among them as one of them. The rope with which he had been tied was left above, lying like a serpent. Quetzalcoatl looked at it for a long while and then said to himself, "The day it rains, feathers will be born on Topiltzin's serpent."

Topiltzin went to his palace without uttering a word. His lips were tight and he was holding back his tears.

❦

On the twenty-sixth day of Quetzalcoatl's fasting, strong winds, raising dust up to the skies and darkening the sun, began to blow.

"The earth and the skies are reuniting," said the sowers of seed. "There is no more rage. Quetzalcoatl has brought the wind. Soon the water will come to bind the earth!" and confidence was reborn.

Above, Quetzalcoatl had cut a shell in half. He placed it in front of him and it became the Jewel of the Wind.

On the fortieth day of Quetzalcoatl's fasting, thick clouds came and the sky rumbled with thunder. And it rained, rained, rained.

The people went up for Quetzalcoatl.

They found him crying. The tears and the rain mingled in his whitened beard.

"You have brought us rain, Quetzalcoatl!"

"It is my son that returns! Bring me the first ear of corn that grows in Anahuac, no matter how small it may be."

When its time came they brought it to him, and he carried it close to his heart, just above the emblem of the Jewel of the Wind.

When they brought him down, to the sound of *teponaxtles* and flutes and canticles of praise, amidst the rain that drenched them all, the Toltecs realized that Quetzalcoatl was becoming old. Wrapped around his body was the rope with which Topiltzin had been tied. Topiltzin understood and he loved Quetzalcoatl again. He joined his retinue of *Cocomes* and was faithful until his death some years later. They also brought the cross down and planted it in the middle of the square once more, and it was adored as the symbol of wind and rain.

In his twenty-sixth year in the land, Quetzalcoatl realized that he had found the way of the Tree of the Universe again.

❧

CHAPTER VIII

The Return of Tezcatlipoca

IN THE OLD CAVES to the north, where thorns grew and frozen winds howled, the wizards were preparing their return to Tula, fifty-two years after Quetzalcoatl's arrival. None of the original ones who had left remained. The ones who had returned when Quetzalcoatl's fate changed were their sons and grandsons. It was during the drought that a Tezcatlipoca, whom they called Titlacahuan, was born. He helped them return. Many children were born in the caves; many came from other places and shared with them the cult of Tezcatlipoca.

"You do not matter, my son," they told Titlacahuan and his brothers. "Your destiny does not matter. You have come to sustain the course of the sun with your enemies' blood, because the sun has enemies in Mictlan and it needs the sacred liquor to recuperate its strength and be victorious. That is the mission and that is the rite. That is man's responsibility. For that reason he is born, and lives, and dies.

The universe is maintained at his expense. His mission is great. His importance is small. He is not the object of creation, but is its sustenance, its minister, without whom the sun ails. Apart from that, nothing matters, nothing counts, human work is worthless. In Tula there is someone who hinders it, the one who threw us out."

In the caves they kept the old gods covered and laid on the earth, as a sign that they were not in their proper place but waiting to return.

But Quetzalcoatl was powerful for a long time and they found no opportunity to throw him out of the land. They did not look for the first chance. It came with Topiltzin's summons and they went to Tula and returned with Quetzalcoatl's firstborn.

But the time for their return had not yet arrived, for one night during the feasts with which they prepared the child's great sacrifice, the very night of the hallucinations, when the earth opened and the sky split in half, when the colors were poured violently into the cry of thunder and the end of the drought came with the rain, Quetzalcoatl's son disappeared with Tatle, the wide-eyed cripple who had introduced the fruits of hallucination among them, the fruits which had been distributed with great sanctimony that night. And they never saw them again. It was established that they had followed the rivers towards the remote lands of the Maya, to the world of the Itzas, where Ku-Kul-Kan arrived from the west. He was a plumed serpent with a message and a mission. But that is a story that is not told here, the story of the twins who arrived at those lands together.

Twenty-six years after the great drought, the wizards achieved their goal and Tezcatlipoca returned to Tula.

During those twenty-six years, Quetzalcoatl was Tula's lord again. In their happiness with the rains, they went to look for him after he had descended the pyramid. And once again, as before, when Ce-Acatl went up to the skies, in a weak voice, and held up by his *Cocomes,* he spoke to the Toltecs, who could hardly hear him through the thunder. Huemac had to repeat his words:

"Ce-Acatl Quetzalcoatl will be the lord of Tula again, according to the will of the Toltecs and by virtue of the wind and the rain. My old age begins and I know my limits. I shall be Tula's lord and I shall seek justice for the Toltecs. The time will come when justice and peace will spread to all the people, but that is not my work and my mission lacks the strength for it. I have fallen many times. My belly has often been pushed to the earth and I have often picked myself up. I have brought benefit and harm, grief and joy. I shall give order and justice to the Toltecs. I will dedicate my days to it. May the Toltecs do justice according to their will. But I shall never again leave this house of the heart of the people. I shall rule from here; I shall not go beyond its doors. I shall remain as a captive of Tula, and Huemac shall now be my voice, as Topiltzin was before. This is the new agreement made among us by the rain, by the ears of the corn."

And with the rain, abundance returned to Tula, and its power and richness grew. Its influence reached the eastern sea, carried from valley to valley through Quetzalcoatl's words. He began to be called the Lord of the Rain and the Son of the Cross and the Wind. It was a new, gentle, and prosperous time which made the Toltecs rich and soft. They were tame and generous, they knew neither hunger nor misery.

But in the north the wizards were conspiring.

Quetzalcoatl's daughter was beautiful. Thirteen years after the end of the drought, she was eighteen. Her beauty was famous throughout Anahuac, but she never left the house of the heart of the people, where she was accompanied by the women of the retinue. Her beauty brought joy to everyone's heart.

At that time Tula's fortune was reaching its highest peak. Quetzalcoatl was wise and just. He had had time to create laws that made life easy and useful. He had had time to establish the rites and the rules for worshipping the precious twin, the wind, the rain, and the cross that tied him to the earth. Feathers, flowers, music, and perfumes were pleasing offerings to the ones who dwelled above. He also had had time to remember grief in abundance, and pierced his legs with the thorns of the century plant and washed off the blood at midnight in a fountain called Xiuhpacoya.

At that time the corn was abundant and the pumpkins large. They grew among the corn stalks, and were so large and thick that a person could carry only one. All the plants were abundant and fully developed. They sowed and reaped cotton of all colors: white, red, flesh-colored, yellow. In Tula many and diverse bird species were created, such as the Xiuhtotl, the Quetzaltotoll, the Zaquen, the Tlauhquachotl, and many other birds sang sweetly. There were cocoa trees of many kinds.

Tulu lacked nothing. The Toltecs were rich and no one suffered hunger or need. When Quezalcoatl wanted to gather the people and make an announcement, the person in charge climbed a tall hill near the city of Tula, called Tzatzitepec, where he proclaimed what Quetzalcoatl ordered in a voice that could be heard for hundreds of miles, as far as the coast. It was the voice of the Tecpan, of the community, that ruled work, feasts, and rest.

The people made Quetzalcoatl's house richer. It consisted of four parts and was round in the middle, like the Jewel of the Wind. It also had four wings: one was made of emeralds, beautiful green stones; another of silver and turquoise; another of white and red shells; and the fourth of all the woods of the land and the feathers of all the birds.

Tecpan had accumulated great riches in Quetzalcoatl's palace. Life was soft and exquisite.

Quetzalcoatl's daughter was beautiful, and in the north the wizards conspired. The fame of the beauty of Tula and of the girl reached them. Although he was older, Huemac had wanted to take her for his wife, as did many leaders and sons of the Toltecs.

But Quetzalcoatl's daughter was not destined to take a husband. She lived happily in the palace of her father, who instructed her in the cult of the Tree of the Universe.

"It is time your daughter had a husband," insisted Huemac. "She must renew the Toltec blood."

"It is her time," Quetzalcoatl answered, "but it is neither her will nor mine. She is happy in her virginity, and as long as she is happy as a virgin, Tula will be too. Do not disturb her serenity. Let her youth sing and dance. Let her enjoy life in her innocence and chastity. She is a girl who sings and dances in front of the Tree of Life."

But one day the girl asked permission to go out of Quetzalcoatl's house for the first time and visit the square, because in it there were merchants from all the regions and great feasts that she had never seen.

And so she arrived in the square, to the surprise and enthusiasm of the Toltecs.

When she arrived at the square, the Magician rose in his splendid virility. He was naked, selling magic herbs that he had brought from the north. The girl was disturbed and embarrassed, and ran back to the house, where she remained, feeling restless. And the women of the retinue noticed it.

After eight days she returned to the marketplace and the Magician was not there. Again she ran back home and her restlessness increased. Eight days went by. She returned and there was the Magician, who again rose, naked, and gave her flowers and herbs. "Take them!" he told her. "You are the most beautiful one! It is fair that you should give your father children. Generation is the triumph of life and race over death and darkness; a crown of flowers in the night, the aroma of herbs in time. Crown yourself and find pleasure!" and he walked down the square until he was lost from sight, while she tried to catch a glimpse of him, holding the flowers and the herbs close to her chest. She went back to her home slowly and sadly, and soon became very ill.

"What ails my daughter?" asked Quetzalcoatl, who missed the songs, the dances, and the soft presence of the girl, who was like a bird. "What is the illness that afflicts her?"

"Lord! The Magician was the cause of this illness. He was naked and your daughter saw him and now suffers from love!"

Quetzalcoatl was greatly disturbed and, speaking no more, secluded himself in his room.

"Great was my sin!" he thought. "I broke the vow of chastity and to make myself immortal I took a woman.

Now, my own flesh suffers because of flesh!" and he suffered without finding comfort in his pain.

His daughter was not getting better. She suffered in silence. She spoke to no one. The songs ceased, the flowers drooped, and the feathers had no glow. But she asked for nothing.

Quetzalcoatl went to see her.

"What ails my daughter?"

"I feel shame and desire, father! I do not understand what is going on inside me. There is great unrest in my soul, and fire in my entrails!"

"What causes it, daughter?"

"A man, lord! A man I discovered at the square! On seeing him, I understood that I was a woman, that I was different, incomplete! And since then I have been invaded by this feeling of dissatisfaction that I do not understand and that burns me."

Quetzalcoatl lost his serenity, and in great rage he said:

"I will not allow desire to disturb your innocence! I do not want you to cease being the girl of laughter, of song, and of dance! I forbid you the thought! You shall not take that fruit! It is not the tree of your life! I do not want it! I forbid it! You must repent!"

"What shall I repent of, father?" she said in anguish. "Dissatisfaction and desire assaulted me roughly and suddenly, when I was least aware. How can I repent if it is like a treacherous blow in my entrails?"

"Then fight! Resist! Struggle!"

"But what must I fight against? What?"

"Flesh! Desire! I have offered your virginity to the creator. I want you to have no guilt."

"Oh, lord!" cried the girl. "What shall become of my

life? What once was innocence has suddenly turned into desire and anguish, and now becomes sin! And repentance, mortification, and the thorns of the century plant will come! And blood, horrible blood will flow to pay a price I do not understand! What can I be guilty of?"

"Of desiring flesh!"

"And why should there be guilt in it?"

"It is the evil, it is the pleasure that stirs your entrails beyond your will!"

"But, lord! I do not understand why good has to lie in grief, and evil in pleasure. Why were we built to be so confused, so contradictory? Better I should remain still with closed eyes, without desiring; but without suffering either. Why did you not teach me that?"

"Because there is merit in it! I have often thought, as you now say, of remaining still, without suffering, without enjoying, without desiring, far from good and evil, without looking for the former or escaping the latter! Still! But my will rebels and wishes to struggle in the world, thinking that only God is beyond good and evil, in total immobility. And then I have fallen and picked myself up again. And it is there, in the risk and the extremes, that I have found merit!"

"Merit, lord! What is the merit of repressing the fire in my entrails when all my body leans toward generation?"

"Offer your generation, your lineage, which is what you most desire, to the lord of merit!"

"But, lord, then the beating of my blood is stopped! My time ends, the flow of my blood in time ends! The blood that came out of you, that has been constructing the universe from the beginning of time, must end with me? Why, lord, why? Am I so great that I deserve the stillness of the blood? Would it not be the most terrible selfishness to sacrifice my generation to merit? Lord! Do I deserve to be the end? Am I not to give my race more possibilities?"

Quetzalcoatl was perplexed at the woman he had discovered in his daughter, and was only able to faintly beg:

"Then do it for me!"

And his daughter, crying, said, "So will it be." And so it was.

But the girl grew worse and her condition became so serious that the women were frightened and decided to speak to Quetzalcoatl, who remained aloof and rigid.

"Lord!" they told him. "The girl is suffering and her illness is serious. There are great troubles in her soul that are struggling with her mission as a woman, and she suffers, and tortures herself!"

"Yes," said Quetzalcoatl, "her illness! Her own illness! It is the illness that has entered her body, against which she must fight. Her will shall triumph!"

"Perhaps, lord, but at the cost of her life! The girl languishes. It is the grief of love, not love itself, that is the illness!"

"It is desire that has fallen upon her innocence, like a jaguar."

"She is a woman, lord! And her youth cries out for generation, which is as strong as a jaguar, and as fierce, and it will kill her if she does not fulfill it! She will dry up!"

But Quetzalcoatl remained firm in his stand. And the girl became worse, and she looked very ill when her father went to visit her. On seeing her, he was frightened.

"You are defeating your body, you are redeeming yourself! You are my honor and my flower!"

"I am defeated! And according to your wishes, soon my

blood will be still. You will be able to offer it, with great generosity, to your lord of merit. I shall soon no longer be your flower, but only the memory of your honor."

"Lord," said the women, "the girl is being sacrificed to words she does not understand: sin, repentance, merit. . . . Her will is tied to you! She will die from two loves, for her race and for her father, crushed between past and future!"

"She shall not die!" Quetzalcoatl replied firmly. "I do not want her to!"

"But she is dying now!"

But she said nothing and for a while there was only silence, a deep silence that afflicted her father.

"Have them look for the Magician," he concluded, and he left feeling defeated and grieved, and did not attend his daughter's wedding, which caused great discontent among the Toltecs.

It was in this way that, through love and generation, Titlacahuan, who was the Magician, sowed the seed of hatred and division among the Toltecs, who were angry with Quetzalcoatl for having given his daughter to a naked savage, a merchant in magic herbs.

The girl became a woman and she bloomed again, but not at Quetzalcoatl's house.

In this way began the return of Tezcatlipoca. Thirteen years later he would achieve Quetzalcoatl's banishment.

CHAPTER IX

❧

The Exodus

TULA'S RICHNESS did not decrease. It was as wide as Anahuac. Its strength, commerce, and goodness went beyond the mountains. Order and the cult of the precious twin made life pleasant.

But a jaguar lurked in Tula's heart, and soon it would devour its entrails. A proud and happy jaguar, as strong and large as Quetzalcoatl, and who, with the strength of his youth, showed his smile and his contempt, much to the hatred of the Toltecs, who had been denied Quetzalcoatl's sweet flower. He went around nearly naked, barely covered by a loincloth. An agile jaguar, who had no rival in the ball game. A powerful jaguar, who always defeated even the strongest and who laughed at everyone.

And the parents, who saw their sons humiliated, dragged through the dust, hurt in the encounter, and mocked in the laughter, hastened to speak to Huemac.

"The Magician is powerful! He is agile in the game and disdainful in his words and in his laughter. He owns the daughter. The Magician comes from nowhere, an herb merchant, as savage as an animal. It is time he showed his worth in things of real risk, and not merely in the ball game. Beyond the snowcapped mountains and the great lake, the people of Coatepec hinder our commerce and rob our caravans. Let him go with our warriors and show his strength and fierceness in battle."

"It is fair," agreed Huemac, who called for Titlacahuan.

"They tell me you are strong," he said. "They tell me you leap for the ball as if you were a jaguar. It is time you leapt in the same way for Tula's enemies. It is time you left your bedroom where you bring happiness to the flower you plucked from the Toltecs. Coatepec shall test the strength of your limbs. You will accompany the warriors."

Titlacahuan laughed disdainfully and merely shrugged his shoulders.

"You shall leave tomorrow," Huemac told him.

"I shall leave tomorrow," consented Titlacahuan.

The expedition left with the merchants. Porters carried the loads. On the way, the warriors conspired to leave him with the porters, weaponless, in the land of Coatepec. As they approached a place where there were beautiful flowers, they gradually left him alone. They withdrew in small groups so as not to arouse fear and suspicion.

He was left alone with the porters, who looked at each other in bewilderment, standing by their loads. Titlacahuan told them, "Soon the people from Coatepec will attack us. The brave warriors of Tula have left to fight against butterflies! No doubt they will return triumphantly, as if they were powerful warriors! Let us prepare for the fight. Chew these herbs that I give you. Great courage will enter the hearts of you carriers, and your arms will become invincible." Startled, they, who only knew how to carry, obeyed him.

"Remain still until I shout, and then we shall attack those who come. In the meantime, don't be afraid."

The people from Coatepec came after having chased a group of Toltecs in vain. They fell upon the goods with great cries of joy, expecting no resistance. When they were most confident, Titlacahuan gave a terrible shout and, springing out like a ball at the Coatepec's leader, broke his head with one blow of his club. Wide-eyed and frothing at the mouth, the porters hurled themselves upon the looters, who were paralyzed with fear and surprise.

The struggle was brief and the victory was quick for Titlacahuan. "Let us tie up the prisoners. Now they will be the ones to carry our load! Let us continue our trip and take the goods to their destination!" In this way they went on and returned to Tula, bringing the warriors from Coatepec as carriers.

Several days earlier the Toltec warriors had returned joyfully. "Titlacahuan shall not return! He is lost in Coatepec; fear stopped him from moving and he did not want to fight! He preferred to stay with the porters. The ball game is different from the game of death with an enemy! Titlacahuan shall not return!" they told Huemac.

And Huemac was happy. He went to Quetzalcoatl and told him: "Your son-in-law, the Magician, was only good at enchanting maidens, playing ball, and laughing. As soon as we wanted him to do something of merit, he became frightened and stayed in Coatepec, lost with the porters among whom he had sought refuge. He was not the one to continue Quetzalcoatl's blood. You committed a great offense against the Toltecs when you gave your daughter to that naked savage. But the people of Coatepec have done justice for Tula!"

Quetzalcoatl, who was growing old and had been ill since his daughter's wedding, said nothing and only stared until Huemac fell silent and left the room.

"Have my daughter come to me!" Quetzalcoatl ordered.

She went to him, more beautiful than ever. He had not seen her since he had consented to the marriage. A great tenderness moistened the old man's eyes.

"Now I realize why my eyes have lost their strength. I need you by me. Since you left, I have felt like a stranger in this land again. I am alone, daughter, and so are you!"

"No, lord, I am not alone. Titlacahuan will soon return and his son lives in my womb."

"A son of yours, my daughter! A son that takes you from me! How far I am from my origin! How thin my blood is becoming! I am an old, remote, ailing man in this land full of sun, a sun my eyes can no longer bear. A son whose father has remained in Coatepec!"

"I do not understand what you are saying, my lord! Titlacahuan will not remain in Coatepec, he will return to see his son. He wants to show him to the people!"

"Huemac has informed me that he has stayed behind with the porters; that he did not want to fight and will not return. Your son will only have a grandfather. An old and withered grandfather who is reaching the end of his time."

"Time goes by for everyone, my lord; but it will not take Titlacahuan, for his mission has not been fulfilled on this earth. He will be your successor! And after him, his son, your grandson. In this way you will be rooted in this land

full of sun. Your grandson will see for you when you no longer exist. This is the way you have chosen to become immortal, through your generation intermingled with the land."

"Titlacahuan my successor! He no longer exists, daughter! Titlacahuan will not return!" She became pale and her eyes were filled with tears, but she soon recovered.

"Titlacahuan will not die, he cannot die! He will soon return, and now I am going to wait for him!"

And she left, leaving the old man immersed in his sadness.

"How far is my origin! How near is my end! My daughter! My son! What has become of my son in the immensity of this land? Tatle! What has become of Tatle in the hostility of this world? Without my daughter! A spore, a seed! How vast, how enormous! How great the burden! How long the road!"

And that day he lacked the spirit to do penance. His heart was heavy with grief and, in the obscurity of the night and the silence of solitude, he wept.

On the following day Titlacahuan returned with his victorious porters armed with the weapons of the people from Coatepec, who carried the load.

It was midday and the sun shone intensely. His arrival was announced from afar with great cries and whistles.

Titlacahuan led them, nearly naked and armed with a club. On his face was the disdainful smile the Toltecs hated so much.

Huemac and his people went to find out what was happening. Surprise, displeasure, and fear captured their spirits. Titlacahuan stood arrogantly in front of Huemac and his retinue.

"Huemac!" he said. "Your warriors are great. It was delightful to see how they ran after butterflies. Their beautiful feathers vied with the flowers and the wings. What a beautiful sight! Their clubs must be full of pollen and the powder of butterflies.

"This club that I carry in my hand is full of the blood of the people of Coatepec. Look!" he cried. And, leaping, he crushed three of the prisoners.

"Huemac! The blood of enemies pleases the gods, but your bland warriors, skillful at chasing butterflies and cutting flowers, do not want to spill it. They abandoned the caravan, and this ball player and these porters were the ones who defended it and who carried out the expedition. This is the way I account for this, Toltecs!"

The people, who were not used to seeing blood, were awed and uneasy. Realizing it, Titlacahuan continued:

"The Toltecs can no longer stand the smell of blood! The Toltecs can no longer face death! The Toltecs no longer know battle, or life, or blood, or death! Let us teach these frightened people the worth of death and the price of blood. Let us do something pleasing to the gods," he shouted. And, together with the porters, he began to kill all of the prisoners, who fled in every direction without defending themselves.

The people were excited and began to shout, "Death! Death!" and in the chaos, without realizing it, many began to help kill the prisoners. The uproar was so great that it reached Quetzalcoatl's home and disturbed his silence and retreat.

"What is happening?" he asked. "What are those cries I hear?"

"Titlacahuan has returned," they told him. "He has brought prisoners and is beating them to death in front of Huemac, who does not know what to do. The people are excited and cry 'Death! Death!' "

"Titlacahuan! Bloody jaguar, demon father of my grandson! I shall go. I shall go to the people. Let my daughter find me at the square," he said, and asked for a whip. He put on his feathered cloak and his great crest and was taken to the square.

When he arrived there, they had already killed all the prisoners and were piling them into a heap. Many Toltecs were helping with the work. The porters danced to the sound of the *teponaxtle* and so did many of the Toltecs. Most of them, however, had retreated and were looking in horror and bewilderment at the terrible sight of the dust, the scorching sun, and the blood that oozed and soon turned into mud. Huemac had left with his people.

Titlacahuan was at his full height next to the pile of dead bodies. They had placed the crown of victory on his head and had dyed his body with yellow and red dust. They had dressed him in cloaks and had adorned him.

There were songs of victory and happiness. "Titlacahuan! Titlacahuan! Titlacahuan!" they cried.

Then Quetzalcoatl arrived. As he was brought in they became quiet until everything was perfectly still. Only the sun shone. The people had not seen him for many years. They knew of his existence; but they did not feel his presence, which still had magic.

His beard was white and, although he was wrinkled, the energy of his features and the power of his eyes were imposing.

Titlacahuan stopped laughing when Quetzalcoatl's daughter arrived, horrified. The old man was still able to stand up straight by Titlacahuan's side. His beard shone as though it were made of silver. The people looked at them in fascination as they faced each other. Quetzalcoatl was the one who broke the silence.

"Jaguar! A stained jaguar! That is what you are, a cursed and cowardly jaguar full of blood and evil!

"Daughter! Your husband has not returned! The one who has returned is this bloody jaguar that I did not know, that entered my lineage through your flesh and your desire! Look at him in front of me stained with the blood of others, with blood dried in his clothes!

"Now I know him. He has the ashen eyes of the old era that wants to return! But it has not come yet! No, cursed Titlacahuan! Quetzalcoatl is still here! You shall not enter Tula! It is not your time!

"I am Ce-Acatl Quetzalcoatl!" he shouted, and he grabbed the whip and began to beat him. Titlacahuan, stunned, tried to rid himself of the cloaks and ornaments that hindered his movements.

Quetzalcoatl's daughter embraced her husband, trying to protect him from the whipping, but only made it more difficult for him to move. The old man went on beating and crying:

"I am Ce-Acatl Quetzalcoatl! This is my time! This is my Tula! Jaguar, cursed jaguar!" And he struck until the couple lay on the ground amidst the dust and the blood of the people from Coatepec.

He stopped when his strength left him, and he fell into the arms of the *Cocomes*. The people reacted and began to sing songs for the plumed serpent, and they praised Quetzalcoatl, who was carried nearly unconscious to his house.

124

Titlacahuan and the daughter remained at the square, surrounded by the porters who carried them far from Tula.

When Quetzalcoatl reached his house, he withdrew to his room.

"Alone, alone again in the middle of the world," he said. "Without a son, without a daughter, without a woman! Tula! My Tula! My work! My blood! Tula!"

And for a long time, he only left his room at midnight to wash off the blood of his sacrifices in a fountain called Xiuh-pacoya.

Fifty-two years after Quetzalcoatl had washed ashore, the terrible year arrived. He was over eighty years old, and he was aged and sad. The people of Tula had not seen him since the day he had beaten Titlacahuan. His presence floated like the climate, like Tula's atmosphere. It was no longer the presence of the man, but of the name. Tula, the city of Quetzalcoatl.

He was old, ill, wrinkled. He had removed himself even from his own loneliness. He could spend many hours completely still. He was like a bubble that floated in a sphere, full of history and with no will. Nothing interested him, not even pain, neither his own nor that of others. He did not want to know about good or bad things. He turned his head when they spoke to him of death, illness, misery, or blood.

With his absence, the Toltecs eased the bonds and the rules. Idleness and laziness softened their flesh and their will. Only Huemac and his group of warriors kept up the unity and the vigor of organization. But they were becoming tired and could not find reinforcements among the people of Tula.

Secretly, Titlacahuan attacked and destroyed, attacked and destroyed. His son, Quetzalcoatl's grandson, already

125

knew how to accompany him. The child's mother, neglected in the caves with the other women of Titlacahuan, was unhappy.

❦

Tula had been split in half. Its wealth was enormous and everyone coveted it. Abundance made the Toltecs bland, and they filled their idleness with more and more complicated pleasures.

At first, among the porters and the laborers, and later among the upper class, it became common to use hallucinating herbs. They were brought from the north, from the Magician, who had returned to his people and was preparing victory by dividing the Toltecs.

He sent his herbs. He sent his people, who addicted an increasing number of people to the cult of hallucination.

The laborers, especially the porters, looked to Titlacahuan for leadership. He was beginning to build a real army composed of Tula's enemies, who coveted its riches. Among them were Chichimecs who practiced the cult of hallucination and even discontent Toltecs who were corrupting Tula's heart more deeply.

Huemac had to face a situation that was becoming increasingly critical. Quetzalcoatl kept to himself more than ever. It was difficult to see him in his house. When someone appeared in front of him, it was hard to make him speak. He remained quiet, staring intensely.

Huemac battled, and for years successfully defended Tula's integrity. Its riches did not decrease and were coveted more and more.

The news that a great attack was being prepared reached

Huemac, and he was afraid because Tula was not aware of the danger. The people were confident, sang, danced, became hallucinated. Huemac, who was beginning to feel the weight of old age, could not arouse the spirit of resistance. He was too rigid and too dry.

He decided to speak to Quetzalcoatl, but even he found it hard to see him. Quetzalcoatl was secluded in the room of feathers. But Huemac went there and told him:

"Lord, Tula is going to be lost! Tula is coming to an end! Titlacahuan is coming from the north with great forces; ours are not enough. Our people are ignorant of the danger and only want to dance and squander the fortune that you created. No one is willing to make the effort, and I no longer have control."

"You are old, Huemac! And so am I! Tula is powerful. She will know how to defend herself!"

"No, lord, she will not! Tula is powerful but she is rotten. Your absence has harmed her. The common spirit that built everything no longer exists. No one thinks about the community. Lord, you must do something or Tula will come to an end! Titlacahuan will come and will demolish the plumed serpent and enthrone Tezcatlipoca."

"Titlacahuan! Tezcatlipoca!"

"You have to do something, Quetzalcoatl! Rouse the spirit of the Toltecs; show them the danger, stir their will! Speak to them, lord! Make them realize that Titlacahuan will upset everything. He will make night of day, death of life. He will devour everything like a hungry jaguar. Tell them, lord! Only you can do something for Tula."

"Huemac," Quetzalcoatl replied, "I have not been able to do anything for a long time. Not even for myself. It is a long time since I have even spoken to a man. I spend long, infinite stretches of time completely still, emptied even of

God's presence! Without pain, pleasure, love, or hatred. Long moments that are only filled by my own absence."

"And Tula, Quetzalcoatl? What about Tula? You are filled with yourself in your absence. What about Tula? Quetzalcoatl's Tula, now threatened by people who are coming down from the north and razing everything in their way? What about Tula?"

"Tula! Huemac! Tula! My life is filled with that name. And who is Tula? None of the ones who were here when I arrived accompany me now! They have all left, they have all died! And there still is a Tula! And she still needs this old foreigner. What can a lonely man do for Tula? Nothing, Huemac! Trust Tula to make her own decisions!"

"But Quetzalcoatl, you must understand! Tula is split in half! The people are in a state of hallucination because of your son-in-law's herbs. Reality has become an uncertain horizon filled with pleasures. Tula is coming to an end, Quetzalcoatl! Tula is coming to an end!"

"I am also coming to an end! The circle will be closed before long. Soon the serpent will bite its own tail!"

"Yourself! Always yourself! Always you!"

"Yes, me! Always me! Huemac! That has been my sin! Quetzalcoatl, filled with Ce-Acatl!"

"You are old, Quetzalcoatl! I would not ask you if I could do something myself. But I no longer can do anything; I have reached my limit. I am defeated if the people do not help me build our defense. I am desperate. I love Tula dearly and I don't want her to perish, I don't want her to become a memory in this land. I don't want her to be a heap of stones and ashes!"

"Stones and ashes!" said Quetzalcoatl. "That is how I feel. As though I were made of stone and ashes."

"Yourself again! Only yourself! What about Tula! Does it not matter?

"Wake up, decrepit old man! I would ask nothing of you if you were not the only one who could arouse these foolish Toltecs! Wake up, old man! Do something for Tula! Wake up, even if you die afterwards! Do something! You are the only one! Are you only able to sit there drooling and staring? Who have I come to see? You are nothing but an empty and wrinkled mask, full of ashes and memories! Dust and ruin, Quetzalcoatl! Old age, old age! Cursed old age that undermines everything, that destroys everything, that ends everything! You are no longer Quetzalcoatl! You are a prostrated old man, filled with self-pity. Tula has lost Quetzalcoatl! There is no more Quetzalcoatl! Let the heavens fall; let the morning star die out! Tula! There is no more Quetzalcoatl!" cried Huemac as he left weeping with rage and desperation.

The old man remained silent for a long while with a bewildered look. Then he sat up slowly and walked towards the door, where there was a ray of sunshine. He looked at his wrinkled hands, with their protruding veins and blotches, their warped fingers.

"Old! I am old! I am old! I am old! My hands and legs tremble. Old! There is no more Quetzalcoatl! Quetzalcoatl is a decrepit old man!" he cried as the *Cocomes* came running toward him. "Quetzalcoatl is an old, trembling man. Cursed be this trembling old man who can do nothing for Quetzalcoatl! Tula is alone! Quetzalcoatl is an old man who feels sorry for himself! Let us cry for Tula! Let us cry, *Cocomes!* How the women and the old men cry! The people from the north are advancing with the step of a jaguar and the panting of a coyote, and here there is only a twisted old man, defeated before the battle! Let us cry for Tula, the city with the old decrepit man!"

"Lord!" said the *Cocomes* to him. "Pull yourself together! You are Quetzalcoatl! You are the lord of this land. Guide your people once more. Speak to them. Lead them to victory. Tula's land is vast and it will not perish. Have pity on Tula! Raise the people on your shoulders once more! Stir the people! Stir the people!"

Quetzalcoatl remained trembling for a long while, and then he finally rose and said: "Ce-Acatl Quetzalcoatl has not passed. Two hearts still beat in his chest. Neither time nor death will defeat a man's will. Quetzalcoatl will lift Tula above time and defeat. Let the jaguars come from the north! Quetzalcoatl shall be here with his whip! Tula shall prevail!

"Tomorrow, have the people gather at the square. Quetzalcoatl shall speak to his people, even if he does so for the last time!"

And the *Cocomes* went to tell Huemac, who was filled with happiness and began to summon the people.

That was the day chosen by Titlacahuan to defeat Quetzalcoatl. He sent for an old man called Ihuimecatl, to whom he said:

"It is essential that he leave his city, where we shall live. He is old now," he declared, "and must desire youth, since he has always wanted immortality. Take him two things, and deceive him with them. Go and give him his body so that, when he sees it in this mirror, he will realize he is old. And give him pulque with hallucinatory herbs so that he will feel young."

Ihuimecatl went there with a great mirror and asked to be led to Quetzalcoatl. "Tell him," he said to the guards, "that in this moment when Tula is endangered, a subject has come to give him his body so that he may lead the Toltecs again."

Quetzalcoatl wanted to see no one, for he was meditating in preparation for meeting the people on the following day. Finally the insistence of the message that someone was coming to bring him his own body broke down the barrier, and Ihuimecatl went to him with the mirror. He entered saying, "My lord, Ce-Acatl Quetzalcoatl, I greet you and come to let you see your body."

"Welcome, old man. Where have you come from? What is this about my body? Let me see . . ."

Ihuimecatl then said: "Lord, I am your subject. I come from the slopes of Nonohualtepetl. Look at your body, lord!" And he gave him the mirror and said, "Look and know yourself! Your body will be reflected in the mirror."

Quetzalcoatl saw himself. He was frightened and said, "My subjects would run away if they saw the wrinkles in my eyelids, my sunken eyes, and my deformed, shrivelled face. My subjects shall never see me again. I shall remain here."

"What are you saying, lord? Feel no distress. The same land that gave you this mirror gives you this juice to make you young. Allow me to summon my brother Coyotlinahual so that this very night he will bring it to you. If you drink it, tomorrow you will be strong and spirited to address your people."

"What you say is absurd! I am old because of the passing of time and there is no juice, no matter how magic it is, that can give me back what time has taken away."

"You must know," said Ihuimecatl, "that there is a point

where the earth and time meet, and it is there that the juice I am offering you springs forth."

"Nonsense!" said Quetzalcoatl.

"It may be nonesense," Ihuimecatl replied, "but it is as truthful as this mirror. What is more, lord, this subject, who brings the truth of your body in this mirror, only thinks of Tula's welfare. What can you lose if you drink the liquid of Coyotlinahual? Are you afraid of dying? You are old, and your heart only awaits the death that is hidden in the shame of your wrinkles. Try it, lord! What can you lose? Tomorrow you will not go out, and you will lose face, and you will lose Tula. Try it, lord! What can an old man lose?"

"So may it be!" Quetzalcoatl said smiling. "Have Coyotlinahual come. What can an old man who has already lost everything lose? Have him come!"

And, in the dark of night, Coyotlinahual went to see him. He brought the drink in the small jugs that were used for honey. Quetzalcoatl was still meditating when they told him that Coyotlinahual had arrived. He was brought in.

"I am Coyotlinahual," he said, "Ihuimecatl's brother. I too come from the slopes of Nonohualtepetl. I bring you the drink of youth that will strengthen your old heart so that you will be powerful once again for Tula's sake."

"I have seen and know a great deal," Quetzalcoatl replied, "but such a drink cannot exist. But I have said I will drink it. What can an old man lose on the day he realized he was decrepit?"

"Try it with your little finger, because it is angry, it is a strong little boy."

Quetzalcoatl tried it with his finger. He liked it and said, "I shall drink three portions."

Coyotlinahual did not persuade him to drink more.

And after Quetzalcoatl had drunk, Coyotlinahual gave all

the *Cocomes* five cups each. They drank and became completely drunk.

❦

Ay! Ya! Nee-ya! Inye! An!

The sun and its colors burst everywhere. His eyes were strong and could take it. The sun in the middle of Teuhtlampa.

Ay! Ya!

Cihuatl! Cihuatl! Come drink with me the liquor of life and immortality!

Ya! Inye! Cihuatl is coming, Cihuatl is coming! Let her come! Ay! Ya! The world is folding and you are in the other half. I am coming! I am leaping! I shall go for you! Ay! Ya!

The colors are strong, but my eyes are stronger. They come from the navel of all things and meet behind the color red. Cihuatl, let us be immortal! I shall keep you alive forever, young! Let us drink! Cihuatl! Let us drink out of the honey jugs. The world is powerful and the sun is enormous. The horizons are filled with every color. The birds are beautiful and their flight is long; it spreads out and it embraces my sphere.

The spotted jaguar who ate my daughter is coming from the north. An enormous, spotted tiger who leaps from the sun. I shall meet it head on! I shall strike him! I am as enormous as Tula's cloak, as a cloud, as the sea. I am green and crimson.

Brother *Cocomes!* Bring me my feathered cloak and my ornaments and my banner. I shall take my son, the little ear of corn with hair of floss, by the hand. I shall take Tatle by the other hand. I shall show the twins to the people!

Acatl, Acatl! Brother, go ahead and announce my com-

133

ing! Have them bring flint. Five pieces of flint will destroy Titlacahuan, the butcher. The sun is beautiful and it warms all the colors of my body. I am strong. I am the one who has arrived.

I am the one I am!

Ay! Ya! In! Ya! Inye! An!

Toltecs who travel through the halves!

I am the one I am!

I am someone! I shall stick five pieces of flint in the body of the jaguar! Five pieces which will break him at night! Five!

Ay! Ya! Inaya! Inye! An! The lord Quetzalcoatl is powerful! He brings wind from the east. He brings rain and separates the halves. I am powerful! Ce-Acatl Quetzalcoatl! Lord of the two halves!

Tula, Tula, my Tula! You shall always be! There will be no stones or ashes. This beautiful warm sun will keep you young forever. Tula! Cihuatl! Daughter!

Wind from the east! The wind is coming!

Ay! Ya!

Cocomes! Let us go up! Let us fly!

We are great, Ce-Acatl, and we are made of stone engraved by the sun, by the wind, and the rain!

The wind is coming! The wind is coming!

Darkness! Yohali Ehecatl!

Wind and Darkness!

The stunned people watched him, with his retinue of drunkards, come out screaming. A grotesque green and crimson mask covered his wrinkled face. Half-naked, the feebleness of his body was apparent. He tried to reach the pyramid, but the *Cocomes* dropped his litter before they got there. Huemac picked him up from the ground and carried him in his arms like a child, knowing that Tula was lost.

Tezcatlipoca had arrived!

For four days, Quetzalcoatl was like the dead. Huemac placed him in a stone box and left him there. He went to prepare Tula's defense. Titlacahuan and his armies were near, and with them were Ihuimecatl and Coyotlinahual, who laughed among themselves as they mocked the old man.

On the fifth day, Quetzalcoatl awoke, and as soon as he was able to speak, he said:

"A bad day away from my house. May the ones who are absent be stirred. May only the one who has an earthen body be and sing."

After Quetzalcoatl spoke, all his *Cocomes* were stirred and began to weep. They sang: "In someone else's house my masters had not yet become rich. Quetzalcoatl's hair has no precious stones. The cross may be clean in some place. Here it is. Let us cry."

But Quetzalcoatl did not cry. He meditated for a long while and said:

"My cross may be clean in some place. I shall go and see. I shall return to the bank. I shall leave, I shall not be the cause of war and destruction. The infinite has completed one turn around itself, and the cycle has been fulfilled. It is time to leave. My father is calling me. I shall go to see if the cross is clean. I shall return to the bank. I shall leave the people, I shall go.

"Close everything."

He left the house of the heart of the people, where Ce-Acatl Quetzalcoatl had lived many years. He lived there. He begot there. He became drunk there. He left, old and defeated.

He ordered his jewels, his gold, silver, turquoise, feathers, and shells to be burned.

And on the night of the fifth day, without being noticed, he left Tula accompanied by five young men. It was fifty-two years since he had arrived at the bank. Tears trickled down his beard.

CHAPTER X

🌺

The Prophecy

AND HE PASSED through Cuauhtitlan, and there he baptized a tall tree, giving it the name "Ahuehuete," the old one. Hay hung from it, and in it he recognized himself.

His *Cocomes* realized that he had gone, and they went after him, and along the way they played flutes and other instruments.

And he passed through Tlalnepantla, where he left the imprint of his hand on a stone, at a place which has since been named Temacpalco.

His *Cocomes* asked him, "Where are you going, lord?"

"I am going to the kingdom of Tlapala, which is in the East. My father is calling me. I am going to him."

"And Tula, what will become of Tula! Who are you entrusting her to? Who will do penance?"

"I have already lost her," Quetzalcoatl replied. "She is no longer in my care. Everything has turned against me. I have lost everything. My time has come and I am going with my father. I am returning to my origin. The serpent is biting its tail, and it is time for it to begin devouring itself."

And he passed by the fountain that has since been named

Coapan (snake water), for he ordered his instruments and his jewels brought by the *Cocomes* to be thrown into it. And he passed through Ixtlaccihuatl and Popocatepetl, the high, snowcapped mountains where the cold killed many of his *Cocomes* so that he decided that only the five youths would accompany him.

And he passed through Cholula, where the people recognized him and asked him to stay with them. But he did not wish to. In his name he left one of the youths who was with him, who practiced the priesthood of the plumed serpent for over twenty years, and introduced and gave prestige to Quetzalcoatl's name.

And in this way, from place to place, from sadness to sadness, he came to the seashore, to a place where a great river, the Coatzacoalcos, flows into the sea. And he did not want to cross it.

"This is my bank. Beyond is the East, my father's house, where I am bound, where I am returning."

It was the time of year when the north wind blows fiercely, and it was very cold.

With the four youths, he started to build a raft made of tree trunks. He wanted the trunks carved to resemble serpents, and it was done according to his wishes.

The night before his departure a harsh wind howled through the trees and blew the sand along the beach.

Feeling so exhausted that he wished to die, Quetzalcoatl lay down with his belly against the ground, opened his arms in the shape of a cross, and kissed and bit the earth with desperation, while his old eyes wept for the last time.

"Earth, my alien earth! I am at your last bank, at my last moments again, as before, as always! Earth and time!

"I shall soon depart, as did Ce-Acatl: he through fire, I through water. Water and fire! From here, with my old eyes closed, I can see everything behind me, but nothing ahead.

"World, my world in rebellion! Son, my son who is lost! Daughter, my daugher who is lost! Woman, my woman who is lost! Tula, Tula! My Tula who is lost! Soon I too shall be lost and I do not know where. I, my self which is lost! Quetzalcoatl has lost his self!

"Everything, everything rebels and turns around itself, around the other, and around myself. My world rebels, my creation escapes me, and the cycle is fulfilled. Everything devours itself. Everything! Time against earth. Stone against nothingness. Plant against stone; beast against stone; man against beast; gods against man.

"And God. Where is God! Who is he who does not rebel? Who is he who is beyond the Omeyocan, beyond the Second Place, beyond all possibilities? Who is the unmovable one?

"God! God! Before you now, I am still myself; I am still someone who still exists. And afterwards, afterwards? And tomorrow?"

There was a long silence when the wind calmed a little, and then Quetzalcoatl cried to the four youths:

"Ce-Acatl Quetzalcoatl. First Cane of the Plumed Serpent. That is I, and I still am!

"Listen! Now I can see ahead.

"My departure is ready and I shall face it alone. I shall soon go to where my father dwells. I shall go alone. My departure concerns me.

"Listen! Listen! And afterwards proclaim it in the land, because my return to the earth concerns the people!

"I shall return! I shall return! I love this alien land, where I have lived, sinned, and redeemed myself for fifty-two years.

"I shall return! My brothers will come!

"Listen! Listen!

"The kings will be vassals!

"Slaves will not exist!

"Your gods have crumbled. You have worshipped them without hope.

"Thus will believe those who worshipped Tezcatlipoca.

"I can see, I can see, I can see now as they will see!

"Listen, listen. Listen to how they will see!

"The ones who worshipped Tezcatlipoca will say, 'This is the word . . . they are coming.'

"All the people are terrified. They are in a state of hysteria, as if the earth moved, as if it trembled, as if everything changed before their eyes. Terror reigns.

"Desperation reigns. They are desperate. They gather to discuss, to weep. They weep in despair, they let their heads droop, they greet one another in tears, they try to comfort each other, they caress the heads of small children, and the fathers say, 'Misfortune, my children! How will you be able to bear this that has come over us? What is in store?'

"And the mothers will say, 'My children! How will you be able to bear the terrible things you will see? How will you bear what will come over us?'

"What will come over us? Who is left on his own two feet? Oh, once I was! My heart is filled with mortal anguish, drowned in fire, which burns me, which bites me.

"They are coming.

"They have arrived.

"They go in crowds, like a flood. They raise whirlwinds of dust. Their iron rods, their shining spears, their curved iron swords, like waves of water, like tambourines. Their iron shirts, their iron helmets.

"And some are completely dressed in iron, which makes them iron men, which makes them glow.

"Pure iron is their war suit, with iron they are clothed in iron. They cover their heads with iron, their swords are made of iron, their bows are made of iron, as are their shields and their spears.

"And their dogs go ahead. They pass ahead of them, they stand in front of them, they lie in front of them. They come panting. Froth drips from their muzzles. And their large dogs, with folded ears, with big tongues dangling, with eyes of fire—of flames, with clear yellow eyes, with sunken bellies. As savage as demons, always panting, always with their tongues dangling, speckled like jaguars.

"And their bodies are wrapped all over. Only their white faces are visible.

"Their faces are as white as lime, their hair yellow; some have dark hair.

"Their beards are long and yellow, too. They have yellow beards.

"They are the sons of the sun. They are bearded. They come from the east. When they arrive in this land, they are the lords. They are white men, the beginning of time . . . prepare yourselves! The white twin of the sky is on his way; the white child is coming; the holy white tree will descend from the sky. He will be announced with a cry a mile before his arrival. Oh, night will fall on you when they arrive! Great gatherers of logs, great gatherers of stones, the white hawks of the earth. They light fire on the tips of their hands, and at the same time they hide their poison and their ropes to hang their fathers.

"Receive your bearded guests who bring the sign of God. They are coming to ask for his offering! The land will burn. White circles will appear in the sky on the day of their arrival. It is coming. The words will be slaves, the trees will be slaves, the stones will be slaves, the men will be slaves when they arrive. It will arrive and you will see it. The world will be filled with sadness. The wings of this land will shudder, and so will the center of this land on the day of their arrival.

"And their servants carry them on their backs, which gives them the height of ceilings.

"Their ranks are formed by horses, their riders on their backs. They carry bells, they come with bells. The bells clash, the bells clash, the horses neigh, they sweat profusely, water drips below them. And the froth from their mouths dribbles to the ground. It dribbles like soapy foam. And when they run, they stamp, making a noise like someone throwing stones. And when they run, they throw up pieces of earth as they raise their front legs.

"Everything bursts. One can see that it thunders, that it flashes with lightning. Smoke extends, smoke is thrown out. Night returns because of the smoke. Smoke lies over all the land, it plunges throughout the entire land until it smells like sulphur, it steals the brain, the heart.

"The saddest star adorns the night's abyss. In the house of sadness, horror makes everything silent. An awesome trumpet sounds, muffled, in the vestibule of the noblemen's house. The dead do not understand. The living will understand.

"Everything seems dead. . . .

"Leave everything! Let it be cursed! What else do you want to do? We shall die! We shall soon be annihilated! We shall soon see death!

"Why do you remain here uselessly? Mexico will no longer be. It has ended once and for all.

"Go, there is no more time.

"That, that will come, that will arrive. And then a new

time will begin. But beyond that I see nothing, I hear nothing. They will come."

Thus spoke Quetzalcoatl, and he said nothing more until the following day.

❦

CHAPTER XI

On the Bank of Stillness

W HEN THE NEW DAY CAME, it was nearly black.
A low, dark cloud lay between the sea and the land. The
wind howled and great waves lashed the beach. Sand and
foam mixed in the same gust.

The strong wind stirred Quetzalcoatl's white beard as he
rose and awoke the youths.

"Only the tree is missing on my serpent raft. Help me
carve it."

And so they did, and when it was finished, they fixed the
cross on the raft. Over it he placed his cloak, which flut-
tered in the wind. He was naked, as when he had arrived.
His old flesh was covered with foam resembling scales. He
said:

"Every moon, every year, every day, every wind, walks
and passes by. And all blood arrives at its place of stillness,
as it arrives at its power and its throne.

"I had a throne and I had power. My blood, which has

run a long time, now wants stillness. My year has arrived, my day has arrived. I am going to the wind, I am going to the sea. I am leaving. I shall depart for my place of stillness. I am already on the bank."

Solemnly, the youths took off their cloaks, which the wind carried as though they were flowers, as though they were butterflies. They kissed Quetzalcoatl's feet as he placed his old and quivering hands on their heads. Three times they tried to launch the raft, and three times the sea brought it back. On the fourth, he asked them to tie him to the cross and, so fastened, Quetzalcoatl, united at last with the Tree of the Universe, left on his serpent raft over a great wave.

Epilogue

WHEN HE HEARD about the arrival of Hernando Cortez's fleet, Montezuma, the lord of the Aztecs, said, "It is our lord Quetzalcoatl who has come, because it was his will to return, to come back, to take his throne again."

When he met Cortez, the unfortunate Montezuma said, "Oh, our lord, you have accomplished your arrival in Mexico, our home, with hardship, with toil. Come and sit on your chair, which I have kept for you for a short while. Your subjects, the kings Izcoatl, old Montezuma, Atzayacatl, Tizoc, Ahuizotl, have left, after keeping it for you for only a short while, and after governing the city of Mexico, under whose protection your people lived. Perhaps some day they will be able to visit their survivors. I wish that one of them could see, with surprise, what has come to me, what I see now, our lord's survival; because I am not dreaming, I am not seeing it in dreams, I have seen your face!"

The companions of Cuauhtemoc, the "Fallen Eagle," the last Aztec king, said, "And when he lowered his shield, after we had been defeated, it was in the year of sign three, and in the count of days, one serpent."

AUTHOR'S NOTE

To investigate the legendary figure of Quetzalcoatl, the Plumed Serpent, I turned to the best-known sources: *Historia de las Cosas de la Nueva España* by Fray Bernardino de Sahagún; *Códice Chimalpopoca* (Annals of Cuauhtitlán); *Indian Monarchy* by Juan de Torquemada; the *Códice Borgia* and, complementally, *Obras Históricas* by Don Fernando de Alba Ixtlizóchitl and *Historia Antigua de México* by M. Veytia.

As basic works I used the *Dinámica Histórica de México* and *Lo Verdaderamente Extraño y Sobrenatural en la Conquista de México*, both by my father, the Engineer José López-Portillo y Weber (published by the Academia Mexicana de la Historia in its Bibliographical bulletin).

As to the figure of Quetzalcoatl, it is known that the name was first given to one of the gods that make up the dualism in the Indian Theogony and that, together with Tezcatlipoca, moves the cycle of a permanent struggle which leads to the universal transformation. This dualism, Quetzalcoatl-Tezcatlipoca, presents similarities with the oriental Mazdaism and with the ulterior expressions of Manichaeism. It can be described as the permanent struggle between two principles, one good and the other evil, with the stirring idea that each one generates its opposite. It is not appropriate now to go into this subject.

We have also found that Quetzalcoatl's name was given to a mysterious character who was present at the tragic Conquest of Mexico, related in a special way to the exquisite and tortured psychology of the unfortunate Montezuma, who awaited his return to hand him the power according to tradition. He was a white man with a black, round beard, big eyes, a high forehead, and quite tall (as Torquemada describes him) who arrived from the East, helped civilize Tula and Cholula, remained in those lands many years and, pursued by priests of another cult (coincidentally that of Tezcatlipoca), fled to the shore. In Coatzacoalcos he prophesied the arrival of white and bearded men from the East, who would come to reconquer. Later, according to some versions, he left by sea on a raft of serpents and, according to others, he threw himself into a bonfire that consumed him while his heart burst and rose to the skies to form the morning star, which is one of the meanings of the word that is translated as the Plumed Serpent.

Finally, we find that the name of Quetzalcoatl was given to the diverse priests who led the cult of this deity. For this reason, the above-mentioned sources relate his deeds, which have become confused in the mass of those attributed to the divinity and to the character to whom we refer.

In this work, we fundamentally deal with a human figure of mysterious character and with the conceptual implications of the philosophical principle with which he is identified in the Indian Theogony.

The sources are especially rich in references to the critical moment of the struggle of the priests of Tezcatlipoca to obtain the expulsion of Quetzalcoatl. Sahagún may be consulted, or, in a very singular way, the beautiful passage of the *Códice Chimalpopoca* which deals with it.

To approach the Chapter of the Prophecy, we resorted to the procedure of integration, consisting of the unification into one body of expression of the prophetical passages of the Chilam Balam of Chumayel, some of Montezuma's expressions of bewilderment, and the account of the companions of Cuauhtemoc quoted by Sahagún, in which is included the story of what happened, impressively told. For the sake of prophecy, we have put them into Quetzalcoatl's mouth before they were really uttered.

On April 14, 1823, after Independence had been achieved, the Supreme Constitutional Congress of Mexico decreed:

> The shield shall be the Mexican Eagle, standing on its left foot on a nopal which is growing out of a rock in a lagoon. It is holding a snake in its right claw, about to tear it to pieces with its beak. This coat of arms shall be trimmed with a border of two boughs, one of laurel, the other of live oak, according to the design used by the government of the first defenders of Independence.

May, 1965
National Place, Mexico